"What did you think you were doing, trying to make a fool of me like that?"

"What do you mean?"

His face was suddenly bare inches from hers, and the sensation of her blood roaring in her ears blotted out any others.

"Why should the tale of that cursed legend even be amongst your notes when I already told you I will have none of it?"

Before Gina had a chance to answer him, his mouth claimed hers.

D1450296

MAGGIE COX loved to write almost as soon as she learned to read. Her favorite occupation was daydreaming and making up stories in her head, and this particular pastime has stayed with her through all the years of growing up, starting work, marrying and raising a family. No matter what was going on in her life, whether joy, happiness, struggle or disappointment, she'd go to bed each night and lose herself in her imagination. Through all the years of her secretarial career, she kept on filling exercise books and—joy, oh, joy—her word processor with her writing, never showing anyone what she wrote and basically keeping her stories for her own enjoyment alone. It wasn't until she met her second husband, the love of her life, that she was persuaded to start sharing those stories with a publisher. Maggie settled on Harlequin Books as she had loved romance novels since she was a teenager and read at least one or two paperbacks a week. After several rejections, the letters that were sent back from the publisher started to become more and more positive and encouraging, and in July 2002 she sold her first book, *A Passionate Protector,* to Harlequin® Presents.

The fact that she is being published is truly a dream come true. However, each book she writes is still a journey in courage and hope and a quest to learn and grow and be the best writer she can. Her advice to aspiring authors is "Don't give up at the first hurdle, or even the second, third or fourth, but keep on keeping on until your dream is realized, because if you are truly passionate about writing and learning the craft, as Paulo Coelho states in his book *The Alchemist,* 'The Universe will conspire to help you' make it a reality."

Other titles by Maggie Cox available in ebook:

Harlequin Presents Extra

ONE DESERT NIGHT

MAGGIE COX

~ One Night In... ~

Harlequin®

TORONTO NEW YORK LONDON
AMSTERDAM PARIS SYDNEY HAMBURG
STOCKHOLM ATHENS TOKYO MILAN MADRID
PRAGUE WARSAW BUDAPEST AUCKLAND

Recycling programs
for this product may
not exist in your area.

ISBN-13: 978-0-373-52853-0

ONE DESERT NIGHT

First North American Publication 2012

Printed in U.S.A.

ONE DESERT NIGHT

To Ruth, who has the soul of a poet and a heart made of love.

CHAPTER ONE

'Who ever loved that loved not at first sight?'

The kingdom of Kabuyadir...

THE sound of crying came to Zahir on the wind. At first he thought he'd imagined it. But when he stepped out onto the balcony overlooking the mosaic-tiled courtyard he heard it again. The sound distracted him from the decision he'd already made to leave the party he was in no mood to attend and go home. He'd gone upstairs to his friend Amir's salon, to steal a few moments to himself away from the mundane chitchat he found it hard to respond to, and very soon he would seek out his host and make his apologies for quitting the party early. In light of what was going on at home, Amir would understand completely.

But now he found himself stepping out into the courtyard, easily bypassing the interested glances that sought to detain him by adopting a detached air that he knew not even the most courageous would disregard. Instead he embraced the kiss of the warm spiced air that stirred his senses as it never failed to do and glanced round him—for what? He hardly knew. Was it a child he'd heard? Or perhaps some small wounded animal? *Or was the gentle sobbing simply an imaginary product of a tired mind and heavy heart?*

The sound of splashing water pouring in a crystalline flow from the mouth of a mermaid into the magnificent shell-like fountain—an impressive centrepiece in the marble-paved courtyard—dulled his hearing for a moment. The only other noise carried on the soft night air was the steady high-pitched drone of cicadas.

Out of the corner of his eye Zahir spied a flash of pink. Narrowing his gaze, he stared hard into a dimmed corner, where there was a stone seat almost shrouded by the shiny dark leaves of a voluptuous jasmine plant. A pair of exceedingly pretty bare feet poked out. Intrigued, he moved forward.

'Who is there?'

He kept his voice low and unthreatening. Nevertheless it carried its usual air of authority. A sniffle, a soft intake of breath, and a long slim arm reached out to brush away some of the protective foliage that more or less kept the stone seat totally secluded. Zahir sucked in a breath.

'It's me…Gina Collins.'

The sweet-voiced announcement was followed by the sight of the most bewitching blue eyes he had ever seen. They all but equalled the light of the moon with their luminous crystal intensity.

'Gina Collins?' The name hardly computed in Zahir's brain. But the appearance of the fair-haired beauty that emerged from her hiding place to stand before him in an ankle-length pink dress with her feet tantalisingly bare could not fail to deeply stir him.

She was a vision of loveliness that no man would soon forget. *No wonder she hid out here, away from view!* Was there a red-blooded male living who *wouldn't* be tempted by such a vision?

Sniffing again, she stoically wiped away the damp smudges beneath her eyes with the back of her hand.

'I am none the wiser about who you are,' Zahir commented wryly, raising a brow.

'I'm—I'm sorry. I'm Professor Moyle's assistant. We came here to catalogue and study Mrs Hussein's books on antiques and ancient artefacts.'

Zahir vaguely remembered the wife of his friend Amir—Clothilde, who was a senior lecturer in art at the university—telling him about her intention to get some help with her library of rare and valuable books. But since his mother had died they had not met, and frankly there had been far more demanding things occupying his time.

'Is the work so distressing that it compels you to hide out here to conceal your dismay?' he mocked gently.

The enormous blue eyes widened. 'Not at all. The work is a joy!'

'Then I desire to know the reason for your tears.'

'I just—I just....'

Zahir found he did not mind waiting for an answer. Where was the need for impatience when his gaze was happy to linger in examination of exquisite features that suggested they had been created by a divine artist who clearly adored her? In particular her lush-lipped quivering mouth.

She sighed softly, and her reply had a tremulous break in it. 'I heard the news today that my mother has been taken ill and is now in the hospital. My employers have very kindly booked me on an early flight in the morning, so tomorrow I'll be travelling back home to the UK.'

A sympathetic wave of compassion and understanding rippled through Zahir. He knew only too well what it was like to have a beloved mother become ill, to watch her health deteriorate day by day and feel utterly helpless to do anything about it. But he was genuinely shocked at how disturbed he was at the notion that this beautiful girl was going home when he'd only just met her.

'I am so sorry to hear your sad news… But I must also confess my regret that you are going home before we have had the chance to become properly acquainted.'

A frown marred her clear brow. 'Even though my mother is ill, I wish I wasn't leaving. Do you think that's very bad of me? I would much rather stay here, if you want to know. I never realised what a painful wrench it would be for me to go, but there's a kind of magic here that's left me spellbound.'

Her response was so surprising that for a moment Zahir hardly knew what to think or say. 'So you like this part of the world? Then you must come back soon, Gina…very soon. Perhaps when your mother is fully recovered?' He folded his arms across his chest and his smile was benevolent and kind.

'I would love that…to come back again, I mean. I can't explain it, but this place has begun to feel more like home to me than my own country. I love it so.'

Her face glowed suddenly, as though lit from within, and suddenly he was not in such a hurry to leave Amir's gathering after all.

'But you must think me very rude for sitting out here on my own when everyone else is inside. Mr Hussein's nephew's graduation is meant to be a happy occasion, and I didn't want to bring things down by being sad. Suddenly I just couldn't seem to contain how I felt. It's difficult to talk to people and be sociable when you're upset.'

'There is not one soul here who would not understand and sympathise with your predicament, Gina. But it is good that you attended the party. It is the custom here to invite as many friends and acquaintances as possible to share in a family's joy when they have something to celebrate.'

'That's what I love about the people here. Family is really important to them.'

'And that is not so where you are from?'

She shrugged and glanced away. 'For some, maybe... but not for everyone.'

'Now I have made you sad again.'

'No...you haven't. I mean I'm sad that my mother is ill, but to tell you the honest truth our relationship is not the loving, affectionate one I could have wished for. My parents are devoted academics...they deal in facts, *not* feelings. To them, feelings just get in the way. Anyway, I've bored you with my troubles for long enough. It was very nice meeting you...but I think I should go back inside now.'

'There is no hurry. Perhaps you would consider staying out here for a while with me? Whatever is taking place in our lives, it is a beautiful night, no?'

Zahir's hand reached out lightly to detain her, and the vivid blue eyes grew round as twin full moons. But, aside from being mesmerised by her startled glance, the feel of Gina Collins's flawless satin-textured skin made him feel almost dizzy with want. He hadn't expected that. It was as though a hot desert wind had swarmed into his bloodstream. He could hardly take his eyes off her.

'All right, maybe I'll stay for just another moment or two. You're right—it *is* a beautiful night.' Folding her arms, she stepped back a little, as though suddenly aware that the distance that separated them was minuscule. 'Are you related to Mr Hussein's family?' she asked quietly, and Zahir saw the flare of curiosity in her limpid blue eyes that she couldn't quite quell.

'I am not related by blood, but Amir and I have been friends for a long time. I have always thought of him as my brother. My name is Zahir,' he volunteered with a respectful bow.

From beneath his luxuriant dark lashes he saw that she blushed. Was it because he had bowed, or because he had only delivered his first name? It might be the way they would have done things in the West if they had met informally at a party, but it was definitely *not* the way men of his rank conducted themselves here in Kabuyadir—especially not when they were destined to inherit the rule of the kingdom after their father!

'Zahir...'

She echoed his name softly—as though it were something wondrous. The sensuous sound caused a cascade of delicious shivers to erupt down Zahir's spine.

'Even the names here have a ring of mystery and magic,' she added shyly.

'Come,' he invited, his blood heating even more at the idea of having her to himself for a while. 'Let us walk together in the grounds. It would be a shame to waste such a glorious full moon on an empty garden with no one there to witness it, don't you think?'

'Won't you be missed if you don't go back inside soon?'

'If my hosts are troubled by my unexplained absence they will be too polite to say so. Besides, I do not have to give an account of my actions to anyone save Allah.'

The woman in front of him fell silent at that. Zahir glanced down at her small slender feet, with toenails painted the same captivating shade as her dress, and a frisson of disturbing awareness rippled through him.

'You will need your shoes if we are to walk together.'

'They're over by the bench.'

Moving back towards the stone seat, with its shield of glossy green leaves and intoxicating white-flowered jasmine, Gina collected her flat tan sandals and slipped them on. When she glanced up again at Zahir, a tendril of golden hair fell forward onto her brow. She brushed it away and smiled. A woman's smile had never had the effect of rendering him speechless before, but it did now. Clearing his throat, he didn't even think twice about extending his hand to take hers. When she wordlessly and trustingly placed her palm inside his Zahir lost all track of space and time, and the grief and turmoil he had been so racked with since his mother had died melted into the ether...

Studying the strong-boned face, with fathomless dark brown eyes and long glossily black hair that was parallel with his shoulderblades, Gina knew she was captivated. With his full-length dark robe—the *jalabiya,* as it was called—and his lean waist encircled by a light brown wide leather belt, he might have been an imposing inhabitant of a bygone court of a wealthy Caliph...a highly trained soldier or a bodyguard, perhaps? He was built as if he could take care of himself and many others besides.

It might be an entirely dangerous action, putting her trust in a man she had only just met, but since such an overwhelming compulsion had never seized her before Gina could only believe it was meant to be. *Kismet* as they often called it in this part of the world. Right then she needed the reassurance of a strong, understanding figure. Something told her that Zahir was a man who *did* understand feelings...the thought was quite intoxicating.

As they walked the meandering paved paths enclosed by a high stone wall that made the building very close to a fortress, with the shining moon benevolently following their progress, she wondered even more how she would endure the stultifying pattern of her day-to-day life when she got home.

When her mother recovered she had no doubt that its pattern would resume—just as though a false note had inadvertently been played, been quickly righted and then forgotten. But Gina couldn't forget or deny her growing yearning to connect with something deeper and more real in her life. She might have fooled herself for a long time that diligent study and adding more and more academic credits to her name, the perusal of dusty old tomes and cataloguing times long past was enough to engage her, to help her feel fulfilled, but since she had come to Kabuyadir she had started to question whether that was the right path for her.

Oh, she still loved her work, but travelling to the other side of the world, discovering a sensual paradise of sights, sounds and scents she had never experienced beyond the descriptive pages of a history book, had forged in her a restlessness and a desire that would never again be subdued.

Her parents—both professors in their chosen fields—had found academic study more than enough to fulfil them and to cement their relationship. Their marriage had come about through mutual interest and professional admiration, but they hardly ever expressed more profound feelings and emotions towards each other. They had raised Gina responsibly, protected her from harm and danger and done all the right things. It had been a given that she be steered towards a career in academia. Rarely had they told her that they loved her...

Now her mother was ill, and she knew in her bones that her father's way of dealing with it would be to retreat even more into the world of the intellect instead of feelings and emotions. Gina would sit awkwardly by her mother's hospital bedside and hardly know what to say or talk about. Yes, her heart would swell with sympathy, but she should have rebelled long ago against the path that had been laid out for her. She should have given academia and books a very wide berth. What had it done for her? She was *dull, dull, dull!* A twenty-six-year-old singleton who lived on convenience foods because she'd never learned how to cook—a pattern she'd inherited from her busily studying parents—and who had never had even one relationship with a man that meant anything.

She had a couple of similarly situated friends, who scorned the very idea of a meaningful relationship because it would undoubtedly be messy and distracting and take their concentration away from their studies. But since coming to Kabuyadir Gina knew that the 'distracting' and totally wonderful concept of a mutually loving relationship was crystallising more and more into a longed-for desire in her heart. So much so that she could no longer ignore it...

'Did you know that the ancient seers and astrologers used to track the destiny of kings through the stars?' Her companion pointed up towards the navy blue bowl of sky that was liberally arrayed with clusters of tiny winking diamonds.

A totally helpless shiver briefly convulsed Gina. Not only were Zahir's darkly handsome looks mesmerising, but his voice was imbued with power and magic, too. Coupled with the dreamlike atmosphere of a still-warm desert night, enchantment was being woven round her heart with delicate but unbreakable gossamer threads that would hold it willing prisoner for a long, long time.

'What about those of us who are merely ordinary, and not kings or queens or anybody special? Do the stars show us our destiny too?'

Gina's heart missed a beat when Zahir captured her free hand and turned both her palms upwards. His dark gaze looked to be deeply examining the fine lines—some with intricate little chains—that mapped her otherwise smooth skin. The playful caress of a soft breeze lifted a fiercely shiny coil of his hair and let it drop back against his cheekbone. Heat invaded her insides like a wild summer storm that plastered her clothes to her frame and ripped her hair free from its usual neat arrangement as though it wanted to free her soul, too.

'I do not believe you are ordinary in any way. Your destiny is beautiful, *rohi*. How could it be otherwise?'

'You're just being kind. You don't know me. Nothing extraordinary ever happens to me…apart from coming here, I mean.'

'It grieves me that you clearly have no sense of your own great worth, Gina…your incandescent loveliness.'

'No one has said such things to me before.'

'Then the people in your life must be blind…deadened to beauty and grace.'

She stared wide-eyed as he bent his head towards hers, with no thought of trying to struggle against a tide that now seemed inevitable. Her sadness and frustration with life was completely banished, to be replaced by the most ridiculous hope and longing as his large strong hands settled firmly on either side of her hips. The intimate contact was like a sizzling brand, burning through the thin material of her dress. When Zahir's mouth descended on hers, his lips were softer than down and more tender and erotic than Gina could have imagined.

He gentled her as though she were a nervous lamb, or a small bird he didn't want to scare or overwhelm with his powerful strength. Beneath his mindful gentle exploration a melting heat drowned her insides in a sea of sensuous honey. The dark trimmed hair that covered his chin and the space above his upper lip was far softer than she would have expected. It was a pleasurable sensation like no other. She would never forget it. As his masculine heat and scent invaded her blood like a drugging opiate, she sensed her knees tremble violently. It shocked her to realise that she wanted more…*much* more of this potent magic he was delivering.

'You are cold?' he asked concernedly, his hands still clasped round her hips as his eyes smiled down into hers.

'No, not cold… I'm shaking because I'm nervous, that's all.'

'I have overwhelmed you…'

When Zahir would have respectfully withdrawn, Gina reached out to lay her hand over his heart. The fine cotton of his robe was as sensuous to the touch as the most luxurious velvet. Beneath it she sensed muscles that radiated the masculine strength and energy of a trained warrior contract. The instant flaring of his inky-dark pupils easily confirmed just how he felt about her touching him. In a trice his arms came around her waist, and suddenly her trembling body was on shockingly intimate terms with the hard male reality of him.

Her thoughts careened into an abyss as pure compelling sensation took over. How could something she'd never even come close to experiencing before suddenly be as essential to her as breathing? If he let her go now she would have to *beg* him to keep holding her. She would risk everything— her pride, her fear, her very *heart*.

Just before his lips claimed hers, the mingling perfumes of jasmine, rose and orange blossom was carried on the air from the flowers that abounded in the garden, heightening moments that would be imprinted on Gina's mind and heart for an eternity. There was a sense of wildness—a raw, elemental hunger about Zahir's passionate kiss. The suggestion of bare control thrilled her, echoing as it did her own helpless urgency and gnawing need. As her mouth cleaved to his, their tongues swirling and entwining hotly, it made her cling to him to keep her balance.

He tore his lips away from hers, his breath ragged, his

glance molten. 'You are leaving tomorrow, and I...' He shook his head, his expression torn. 'I do not know how I can bear to let you go.'

'I don't want to go...but I have to, Zahir.'

'Must we part this way? On my honour, Gina, I have never felt like this with any other woman before... As if... as if she were a part of me that I never even knew I had lost until I saw her.'

Devouring him with her eyes, Gina felt her heart squeeze with anguish at the mere thought of them being separated. *Would people judge her as heartless—as cold and unfeeling—because she preferred to stay here with Zahir instead of going home to see her sick mother?* Right then she didn't care. How could she when she'd been so bereft of love—of warm, human touch—for too long? Why should she feel guilty and weigh herself down with painful responsibility when his impassioned confession echoed the heartfelt yearning in her to reach out for something wild, warm and wonderful beyond imagining?

'You are staying in one of the houses in the grounds, I presume?' He drew her with him beneath the shelter of a shady tree, glancing behind them as if to check whether they were being observed. But the shadowed fragrant garden was empty and still except for the hypnotic drone of the cicadas and the soft gushing of the water fountain.

Worrying her lip with the edge of her teeth, Gina nodded.

'Can we go there?' Zahir's thumb was stroking back and forth across the fine skin of her fingers, and the tension between them grew tight as a bowstring on the verge of snapping in two.

'Yes.'

They moved in silence towards the end of the garden, where a vine-leaved arbour led onto another paved area.

There sat a long, low adobe-style residence, with an arch-shaped entrance like the Ace of Spades. It was decoratively outlined by ornate gypsum, its walls inset with traditionally narrow windows to keep out the glare of the heat. Within the garden was a tranquil pond and a beautiful mosaic-tiled fountain. Because rainfall was more abundant up here in the mountains greenery thrived, and heavily perfumed blossoms were everywhere. The temperature was not so fierce, either. Occasionally they were blessed with distinctly cool breezes.

About two hundred yards away, secluded by magnificent date-palm trees, was another building. This was occupied by Gina's boss, Peter Moyle. But Peter was still at the Husseins' party, and she and Zahir could slip inside Gina's lodgings unnoticed.

Feeling daring and wild, as well as a little afraid, she knew her behaviour was unlike any she had displayed before. She'd thought of herself as staid and boring for so long that the uncharacteristic impulse to reach for something she yearned for with all her heart and not fear the consequences was utterly exhilarating. Reaching for the slim iron key that was in the pocket of her dress, she inserted it into the lock and gave it a twist.

The Moroccan lanterns she'd left burning softly cast a seductive glow round the wide decorative vestibule that led into the main living area. When Gina started to move in that direction Zahir caught her by the waist, and what she saw blazing in his eyes smothered every thought in her head to silence.

'Where is it that you sleep?' he asked, his voice low and imbued with the sensuous drugging heat of the desert itself.

Slipping her hand into his, she led him into the blissfully cool bedroom, with its marble floor, and to the bed that was graced with a silken canopy the colour of a dramatic burnt orange and red sunset. Brass wall lights and another softly glowing lantern rendered the interior warmly intimate.

Stepping in front of her, Zahir cupped her face between his hands—hands that were warm and capable and big. He had the hands of a protector, for sure. And his gaze…his steady dark gaze…was a benevolent silky ocean that Gina would willingly submerge herself in for the longest time.

Inside his chest, Zahir's heart drummed hard. His confession that he had never wanted a woman this much before was perfectly true. How could attraction be so instant and so…so *violent*? he mused. His every sense was irrefutably held captive, and he could barely think, let alone hope for some understandable explanation. He found himself intimately examining the arresting features before him. In contrast to the brightness of her golden hair, Gina's arched brows were dark and generous. They raised her exquisitely formed features to a visage far beyond merely pretty, stamping them with a beauty that was hard to forget.

It was, Zahir thought, perhaps the only night they could be together for a long time. Who knew how long Gina's mother would be in the hospital? How long before her lovely daughter could return to Kabuyadir? The idea made his insides lurch painfully. Why had fate brought him this treasure only to rip it away from him so soon…*too* soon?

'I never expected…'

Gina sucked in a breath, her lips visibly trembling, bringing home to Zahir how nervous she was. How to convey without the use of words—words that would surely be woefully inadequate—that he would never knowingly cause her hurt or bring her shame? Those same reasons had made him check to see if they were being observed just now in the garden. He would willingly shoulder all the blame if someone were to even *think* of judging her.

'Neither did I, *rohi*.' He laid the pad of his thumb across her plump lower lip and stroked it. 'And if all we are destined to have together for a while is this one night…then I will make sure it is a night that our bodies and souls will never forget. That is a promise I make to you straight from my heart…'

Three years later…

'Dad, are you there? It's only me,' Gina called out after letting herself in with her key.

She gathered up the stack of letters on the mat inside the door, frowned, and made her way along the rather gloomy hallway to the back of the three-storied Victorian house, where her father had his study. He was hunched over at his desk, staring at what looked to be an aged, yellowed document. Just then, with his mussed greying hair and his too-thin shoulders in a blue unironed shirt, he seemed not just preoccupied and isolated, but sad and neglected, too.

In Gina's heart a pang of guilt mingled with her sorrow. She'd been working hard at her new job at a prestigious auction house, had rung him nightly, but hadn't called in for a week.

'How are you?' Leaning towards him, she brushed the side of his unshaven cheek lightly with her lips.

He stared up at her with shock in his eyes…just as if he'd seen a ghost. Then he grimaced and forced a smile. 'I thought you were Charlotte. You're looking more and more like your mother every day, Gina.'

'Am I?' The comment surprised her, and made her heart skip a beat. It was the closest thing to a personal remark Jeremy Collins had made to her in weeks. He particularly avoided mentioning his wife, Gina's mother, if he could help it. Her death three years ago had hit him much harder than she'd ever envisaged it would. Gina was disturbed that he should bring her up now.

'Yes, you are.' Shrugging his shoulders, Jeremy laid down the yellowed document and tried for a smile. 'How's the job going at the auction house?'

'It's really testing my mettle, if I'm honest. I mean, just when you think you've got a handle on something you discover there's so much more to learn.'

'You sound as if you're learning some valuable wisdom along the way as well.'

'I hope so. No matter how many diplomas I've succeeded in getting, I still feel very much a junior in this trade, Dad.'

'I understand, dear. But don't be in such a hurry to get somewhere. This "trade," as you call it, is a lifetime's passion for most who enter into it, and you never stop learning and discovering things you didn't know before. You're still so young… How old? Remind me?'

'Twenty-nine.'

'Good God!'

His exclamation made Gina giggle. 'How old did you think I was?' she playfully challenged him. At least he wasn't looking so down and distracted now, she noticed.

The greying eyebrows made a concertina motion. 'In my mind I always remember you at round about five years old…reaching a sticky exploring little hand towards the papers on my desk. Even then you had an interest in history, Gee-Gee.'

Dumbfounded, Gina stared hard, 'Gee-Gee?'

'It was my pet name for you. Don't you remember? Your mother thought it highly amusing that a distinguished professor of antiquities and ancient history should have the imagination to come up with something like that.'

'Here.' There was a lump in her throat the size of an egg as she handed him the letters she'd found on the mat.

'What's this?'

'Your post…looks like it's been accumulating for days. Why didn't Mrs Babbage bring it in for you?'

'What?' The pale blue gaze was distracted again. 'Mrs Babbage resigned last week, I'm afraid. Her husband had to go into hospital for a major operation and she wanted to be able to visit him as often as she could. Under the circumstances, she couldn't keep her job here. Anyway, I shall need to interview for a new housekeeper.'

Reaching out her hand, Gina laid it briefly on his shoulder. She was shocked to feel how little flesh covered it beneath his shirt. 'That's the third housekeeper you've lost in a year,' she commented worriedly.

'I know. Must be my sparkling personality or something'

Ignoring the droll reply, Gina gazed at him, seriously concerned. 'What have you been living on for a week? Not much, by the looks of it. Why didn't you tell me about this when I rang you, Dad?'

For a moment the expression on her father's long thin face reminded her of a small boy who had been reprimanded by a teacher and told to stand at the back of the class. The lump inside her throat seemed to swell.

'Didn't want to worry you, dear… You're not responsible, you see. It's my own stupid fault that I never took the time to learn how to cope with the domestics… Head always in some book or other, you see. Since your mother went I don't seem to have the heart for much else. People thought I was a cold fish when I didn't cry at her funeral. But I cried inside, Gina…' His voice broke, and moisture glazed the pale, serious eyes, 'I cried inside…'

She hardly knew what to say—how to respond. It was as

though a stranger sat in front of her—not the remote, self-contained, preoccupied man who was her father. The man she would have been hard put to it to say had any feelings at all.

Patting his bony shoulder again, she gave it what she hoped was a reassuring squeeze. 'Why don't I make us both a nice cup of tea? We'll have it in the living room, then I'll nip out to the supermarket to get you some supplies for the fridge.'

'Are you in a hurry tonight, Gina?' The moisture beneath the pale eyes had been dashed away, and now his eyes glimmered with warmth…affection, even.

'No, I'm not in a hurry. Why?'

'Would you—I mean could you stay for a while? We could—we could talk. You could tell me a bit more about your work at the auction house.'

Was this some kind of breakthrough in their difficult and sometimes distant relationship? Why now, when it had been three years since she had lost her mother? Had it taken him that long to realise that he'd really loved Charlotte? That he loved his daughter?

Gina didn't know right then whether she felt hopeful or angry. Shrugging off her raincoat, she folded it over her arm, then crossed to the still open study door. 'I don't have to rush off. I'll go and put the kettle on. Why don't you go into the living room and make up the fire? The house is chilly.'

In the kitchen, staring at the peeling paintwork and the cupboards that she guessed were as bare as Mother Hubbard's, Gina filled the kettle at the sink and plugged it in. Before she realised it, her eyes were awash with tears. To find her father dejected, sad and reminiscing about her as a child was disturbing enough, but earlier on today her senses had received another jolt.

She'd been asked to work with a team of researchers on the provenance and history of a valuable jewel from Kabuyadir. Just the name of the place had the power to arouse the most potent of memories, and make her ache for a man whose skin was imbued with the scent of the desert, whose eyes burned with a passion that had consumed her from the very first glance—a man Gina had reluctantly had to say a premature goodbye to that magical, unforgettable night three years ago, because she'd been returning to the UK to see her mother in hospital.

When Charlotte Collins had passed unexpectedly away shortly afterwards, it had knocked Gina for six. It had also heightened her overwhelming sense of responsibility towards her father. So much so that when Zahir had rung her for the second time from Kabuyadir, in the days following the funeral, she had determinedly decided to put their night of wonderful passion and *kismet* behind her to focus instead on an academic career. Her father had told her that her mother would have wanted to see her make a resounding success of it.

With tears burning her eyes, and a lump in her throat the size of Gibraltar, Gina had declined Zahir's heartfelt pleas to return to Kabuyadir soon and told him she was sorry— what had happened had been wonderful, but the idea that they could be together wasn't remotely realistic. Now that she was back in the UK it was her career that had to be her focus, not some love affair she'd be completely foolish to trust in.

Even as she'd been speaking she'd felt as if a stranger had taken over her body and mind...a *despondent* stranger who certainly didn't believe in love at first sight or happy-ever-after. When more time had passed, she'd continued quietly, he would see it that way, too, she was certain.

Zahir's parting words had broken her heart. *'How could you do this to me, Gina...to us?'*

CHAPTER TWO

WALKING into the serene courtyard garden, where the air was heavily hypnotic with the perfume of drowsily alluring blossoms, Zahir saw his sister sitting on the long wooden bench beside the pretty ornamental pond. Her sad gaze was as far away as ever, in a land he couldn't reach.

Beneath his black *jalabiya*, Zahir's taut abdominal muscles clenched uneasily. They had always been close, but since Farida had lost her husband Azhar six months ago she had become withdrawn and uncommunicative, and all the joy had vanished from her almond-shaped dark eyes. Would he ever see it again? He hated to think he might not. There wasn't anything he owned that he wouldn't give to see her happy once more. With their parents gone all they had now was each other...

'Farida?'

Her glance barely acknowledged him before returning to its dreamlike examination of the pond.

'I am going into the city today on business, and I thought you might like to go with me? We could stay overnight at the apartment and have dinner at your favourite restaurant. What do you think?'

'I would rather stay here, if you don't mind, Zahir. I don't feel like facing the city crowds today—even if it is only from behind the tinted windows of your car.'

Zahir's responding sigh was heavy. Since he had lost his father and inherited rulership of Kabuyadir he was looked to—and indeed *expected*—to dispense wisdom, guidance and help to the people of his kingdom. But apparently not to his own sister. As far as that aspect of his rank and power was concerned he was all but useless.

'What will you do with yourself here all day on your own?' He tried hard, but couldn't quite keep the frustration out of his voice.

She shook her head and would not look at him. 'I will do what I usually do. I will sit here and remember how happy I was with Azhar, and know that I will never be happy again.'

'You should have had your marriage arranged, as is the custom!' Zahir flashed irritably, pacing the stone flags surrounding the pond. 'Then it would not have been such a blow to you when you lost your husband. This—this marrying for love was a mistake. Has our tragic history not taught you that?'

Now Farida *did* look up at him. 'How can you say such a terrible thing, Zahir? Our parents did not have an arranged marriage, and they knew the kind of joy and happiness that made them the envy of everyone. Have you forgotten how it was with them? Father told me once that loving our mother made him feel more complete and content than anything material this world could ever do.'

Folding his arms across his broad chest, Zahir came to a standstill beside her. 'And he was a broken man when she died. So broken that he followed her soon after. Have *you* forgotten *that*?'

'You have changed, Zahir, and it worries me just how much,' Farida told him sadly. 'Your rule of Kabuyadir is exemplary, and would have made Father proud, but your rigid rule over your heart has made you cold and a little bitter,

I think. Remember the prophecy of the Heart of Courage that has been in our family for generations? It says that all the sons and daughters of the house of Kazeem Khan will marry for love—not for strategic or dynastic alliance. Remember?'

Knowing he had already set plans in motion for the sale of that cursed jewel, Zahir flinched a little. 'Yes, yes—I remember. But I personally will *not* be adhering to that. In fact my business today involves preliminary negotiations with the Emir of Kajistan for the hand of his daughter in marriage. She has just turned eighteen, so is eligible. It is a good match, Farida…sensible.'

'You plan to marry the dull-witted plain daughter of our neighbour? Are you mad? She will drive you crazy in a matter of hours, let alone days!'

Her brother's eyes narrowed. 'Yes, but because it will be a marriage of convenience I am not bound to spend every waking hour with the lady. She will have her own interests and I mine.'

'And what will they be, I wonder? Regularly visiting the beauty parlours in the big city in the hope that they will have some transformative elixir that will render her beautiful? I believe in the power of magic, brother, but I would have trouble believing in a magic as powerful as that. It would be like hoping for a powder to turn a mule into the most elegant of Bedouin thoroughbreds!'

'Farida!' Zahir was quick to show his displeasure at this insult to his potential bride, but underneath his admonishing glare his lips twitched in amusement. It reminded him of how mischievous and playful his sister could be. He threw her a final beseeching glance. 'Won't you come with me today? When my business meeting is over I would really welcome your company.'

'I am sorry, Zahir. But I have given you my answer and

prefer to be left here alone. However, I pray that you come
to your senses and forget about making such a soulless
marriage with the Emir's daughter. Have you never wanted
to fall in love like our father did? Like our ancestors did...
like *I* did, too?'

A pair of incandescent long-lashed blue eyes flashed in
Zahir's mind, instigating such a powerful longing inside
him to see their owner again that he fought to contain it and
return to cold, hard reality instead. Icy reason told him that
even to entertain such a hurtful memory was to go down a
road made impassable by bitterness and disillusionment.
The woman had rejected his entreaty to return to Kabuyadir
and his arms outright. Never again would he risk his heart
that way, or give his trust to a woman.

When he finally spoke his voice was gruff. 'The premise
is pointless, and I am not a masochist willing to experience
more pain and anguish than I have endured already. No,
that is not a path for me. Now, can I bring you anything
back from the city?'

'No, thank you. Just go safely and return home soon.'
With the barest glimmer of a filial smile, his sister returned
to her lonely musing over the clear still pond at her feet.

Gina had fought hard in her case to win the right to travel
to Kabuyadir and examine the jewel she and her colleagues
had been researching these past few weeks, and she'd won
the battle. Still, it was a double-edged sword to go back
to the place where she'd experienced her greatest joy and
deepest pleasure and know that she'd foolishly trampled
the chance she'd had to be with the man she loved into
the dirt.

Now, as her colleague Jake Rivers drove them to the
airport, she stared out of the passenger window of his small
Fiat in silence, reflecting on returning to the place where

she had lost her heart to a handsome, enigmatic stranger—a stranger she had dreamt about almost every night for the past three years. The dreams endlessly replayed that incredible night they had spent together under the desert stars.

'*Zahir.*' She murmured the name softly.

Not for the first time she wondered where he was and what he was doing. Was he married to a girl from his own land now? Was he father to a child that played happily at his feet and made him ache with pride? *Did he ever think of Gina and remember the incredible instant connection they had shared?* Or had he relegated it to a moment of madness he regretted because she'd callously rejected his invitation to return in preference to forging ahead with her career?

Chewing down hard on her lip, she felt her insides flip in anguish. She'd wanted to make her father proud and honour her mother's memory, but in doing so she'd sacrificed perhaps the one real chance of happiness she would ever have. Bad enough that she hadn't seen Zahir again after that one night, but to think that he might despise her for the choice she'd made was a psychological blow beyond cruel. *Please, God, no...*

'What did you say?'

Realising she had spoken out loud, Gina glanced round at her erudite bespectacled colleague, her face hot. 'Nothing... just thinking aloud for a moment.'

'I can't believe you've been to Kabuyadir before. What was it like?' Jake asked conversationally as he negotiated the route to the long-term car park.

Shutting her eyes for an instant, Gina felt it all come flooding back—the scent of exotic spices and incense, the sound of languages with their origins in ancient Persian and Byzantine empires, the vibrant glowing colours of the wares in the marketplace, and the fragrant perfume of the Husseins' garden that was hypnotically carried on the sultry wind.

Most of all she recalled Zahir's strong-boned face, and eyes so chocolate-dark that one arresting glance had been enough to steal her heart and keep it his for ever...

'Whatever description my words could give you wouldn't do it justice. Why not just see for yourself when we get there?'

He sent her a smile as he parked. 'All right, then. I will. By the way, how's Professor Collins doing? What's he working on at the moment?'

Jake's tone had both admiration and curiosity in it, and Gina kept her expression as neutral as possible. Usually she tried to stick to a policy of keeping her personal life well out of her professional one, but she supposed it was inevitable that her ambitious young colleague would be curious. He had confessed to her from the very first that he was Jeremy Collins's 'greatest admirer' because of what he had achieved in his long and distinguished career.

'I have no idea what he's working on, but he's been a bit under the weather lately, to tell you the truth. Thankfully I found him a new housekeeper, who seems very thoughtful and caring, so I'm trusting he'll be okay while I'm abroad.'

She hoped she didn't sound as anxious as she felt. Suddenly her father seemed worryingly forgetful and fragile, and her heart bumped a little beneath her ribs when she thought of him struggling with the daily chores most people found easy.

That was why she was so thankful that she'd found Lizzie Eldridge. As his new housekeeper she would be just perfect. A forty-something single mum of an eleven-year-old, she was down to earth and immensely practical, as well as kind. She and Gina's father had hit if off straight away. He was in safe hands, she thought as she wheeled her suitcase across the concrete to the dropping-off point for the bus that would take them to the airport entrance.

'I can't wait to see the jewel "in the flesh" as it were,' her companion enthused as he walked beside her. 'That central diamond—or *Almas*, as they call it—is quite something. The owner can't be short of a few quid, seeing that he's the local Sheikh an' all, so I wonder what's made him think of selling it?'

'That is surely none of our business?' Gina responded with an arch of her brow. 'All I know is that it's a tremendous privilege to study the history of such a jewel…a jewel that research had corroborated hails from seventh-century Persia.'

'Hmm…' Unrepentant, Jake grinned. 'I wonder what he's like, this "Sheikh of Sheikhs" as he's known? Can you believe we've been invited to stay at his *palace* instead of some local flea-bitten hotel?'

'I'd be careful about coming out with things like that when we're in Kabuyadir, Jake. It might be construed as disrespectful…which it *is*.'

'Have you always been such a good girl, Gina?' The hazel eyes behind the fashionable ebony glass frames were definitely speculative as well as teasing. 'Don't you ever let your hair down and just, well…*misbehave?*'

It was such an outrageous comment that Gina sensed herself flushing hotly. She had 'misbehaved' once—in Kabuyadir, as a matter of fact—but at the time it hadn't seemed at all as if she was doing wrong. Under the circumstances it had seemed like the most natural thing in the world, because it had been purely instinctive and *right*. She certainly didn't regret what others might regard as her moment of madness if they knew about it. Not even *once*.

Running her hand over her tidy French pleat, she felt the leap of intense longing to see Zahir again almost overcome her. 'I'm not perfect, Jake. I have my foibles just like anyone else. Let's leave it at that, shall we?'

There were moments in a person's life when the sheer wonder of a sight left an imprint on the heart and mind that would never be erased. Stepping into the vast mosaic and marble courtyard of Sheikh Kazeem Khan's ornately gilded palace was one of them.

Shielding her gaze against the dazzling sunlight that rendered the tall golden turrets almost impossible to look at for long, even with her sunglasses on, Gina glanced over at an equally mesmerised Jake and shook her head. Words seemed unnecessary.

Lifting her face up to the skyline again, she noted the impressive stone-built watchtower, hovering even higher than the golden pinnacle of the roof. Once upon a time this palace must have been the most intimidating and impenetrable fortress. It wasn't hard to imagine what it must have been like then. From the outside it appeared as if twenty-first century modernity had barely touched it at all.

A slim-built young man with watchful amber eyes, dressed traditionally in a *jalabiya* and a headdress with a colourful *agal* rope securing it round his head, stood waiting patiently as the two Europeans ogled a sight that for him was no doubt commonplace. His name was Jamal, and he was proud to call himself a servant of Sheikh Kazeem Khan, he told them. He had met them at the foothills of the city, where the taxi that had waited for them at the airport had left them, and had then accompanied them up the mountain in a cable car. From there, a comfortable horse-drawn buggy, with ravishing silk curtains and cushions, had transported them to the palace.

Gina was tired, travel-worn and melting in the heat, yet an undeniable excitement thrummed in her veins, making her not want to miss anything if she could help it.

'We must not linger here in the afternoon heat. We should go inside now. This way.' Jamal made a sweeping motion towards a vaulted sandstone passageway. 'Another servant will show you to your rooms, where you can rest for a while. Then, later, you will make preparations to meet with His Highness.'

Gina's tiredness vanished completely when she was shown to her guest quarters. She'd been absolutely charmed by the comfortable adobe style house that she'd lived in when she'd stayed with the Husseins, but *this*…this was like walking into the sumptuous boudoir of an eastern princess. The furnishings were lush, with ravishing silk brocades of every imaginable hue and colour, and floor-to-ceiling voile drapes fell in a sensuous sunburst from two slim windows. An azure-coloured blind was partially unfolded behind the curtains, to keep out the heat and glare of the sun, and the floor was made from blissfully cool white marble. A generous-sized Persian rug picked out in sensuous gold and bronze threads was spread out at the foot of the bed…*the bed*.

If Gina had been inclined to write poetry she would have composed a veritable sonnet to such a bed. It was vast in every sense, with the broad-clawed feet of a sphinx and intricate Arabian carvings inlaid in a rosewood head-board that appeared magical and ancient at the same time. It practically drowned beneath a sea of silk and brocade cushions of every conceivable shape and colour.

Throwing herself down amongst them, she sighed with pleasure. A delicious if bittersweet daydream about Zahir drifted into her mind. *Was there some way she could get to see him?* she wondered. *Was she crazy to even hope he might agree to a meeting?*

She would have broached the subject to Mrs Hussein on that morning before she'd left for the airport to return home—asked her hostess if she could elaborate on who he was and where he lived. But Clothilde had seemed busy and preoccupied, and it just hadn't felt right or proper to ask about the charismatic male guest that Gina knew simply as Zahir.

He'd left early the next morning, even before she'd risen to dress for the airport. His parting embrace had filled them both with intense longing all over again, but she'd given him her phone number and he'd promised to call her the very next day. It had been the hardest thing she'd ever done to kiss him goodbye and then watch him walk away, with the only remaining evidence of his presence the scent of warm aroused male he'd left on her body and the tingling ache between her thighs. She had surrendered her innocence to him—surrendered it with full heart and a fervent pledge to love him for ever…no matter what.

It was said that a woman never forgot her first love. In Gina's case her *only* love. That was why she could never give up her precious memories of that night. But she'd made sure all she would ever have was memory when, incredibly, she'd rejected Zahir's invitation to go back to Kabuyadir and be with him. Even now she couldn't believe she'd done it. Grief over her mother and worry over her father must have temporarily made her lose her mind. The thought of the pain and disbelief in Zahir's proud voice had gone round and round in Gina's head for three impossible years.

Turning her face into a plump silken pillow, she felt stinging tears of regret and longing wash into her eyes as she whispered his name…whispered it like a *prayer*…

* * *

At last Farida had retired to her quarters, and Zahir could safely entertain his guests from England. She would only become agitated and tearful if she knew of his intention to sell the Heart of Courage—the jewel that she seemed convinced was possessed of some kind of prophetic power when it came to their family's marriages. But when sufficient time had passed and she was more like herself again he was certain he could persuade her that the sale was for the best.

They had had a tumultuous time of late. Their parents had left this world one after the other, and then Azhar—Farida's husband—had lost his life in an automobile accident in Dubai. The only thing his beloved sister needed right now, Zahir believed, was peace and plenty of time to heal. The presence of a family heirloom that he privately thought of as a curse would not help her achieve that. And for him it would only act as a painful reminder of all he had lost. It mocked his once fervent belief in it himself. *He'd rejected the prophecy when the woman he had fallen in love with callously turned down his plea for her to be with him...*

The money he received from the sale of the jewel he would give to Farida, to do with what she willed, he decided. *He certainly didn't need it.*

There was plenty of evidence in palace records to vouch for the authenticity of the jewel, but as he planned to sell it abroad he'd needed to have that evidence corroborated by a respected independent source. The auction house in Mayfair had an internationally respected reputation. His two guests were a male historian and his female colleague who specialised in the study of ancient artefacts. Zahir hadn't seen their names—he'd left the details to his personal secretary and lifelong friend Masoud, who had now unfortunately been taken ill—but he had ensured that out of respect and deference the female would have one of the best staterooms in the palace.

Now, as he waited in the main salon where he received visitors, he didn't know why but an odd sense of foreboding gripped him. Telling himself that he was becoming as bad as his sister, believing in all kinds of supernatural phenomena, he impatiently shook away the unwelcome frisson that shivered down his spine. Lifting the sleeve of his *jalabiya,* he glanced down at the linked gold watch circling his tanned wrist. The ornate twin doors at the end of the long stately room suddenly opened and his servant Jamal appeared.

'Your Highness.' He bowed respectfully. 'May I present Dr Rivers, and his colleague Dr Collins?'

Already walking forward with his hand outstretched, Zahir felt his footsteps come to a frozen standstill. Beside a slim-built man with sandy-coloured hair who wore glasses stood a woman with elegantly upswept blonde hair, her svelte figure dressed in a long, flowing silk kaftan in stunning aquamarine. But it was her beautiful face and riveting long-lashed blue eyes that made his heart almost stop.

Gina… Was he dreaming?

He could hardly believe it. Everyone was staring at him, waiting for him to speak, but just then to him that was akin to growing wings and flying. Clearing his throat, Zahir moved towards the man first. Even as he was shaking his hand his mouth dried and his chest tightened. He knew he would slip his hand into Gina's next. She was clearly as shocked and startled as he was. Her cool, slim palm trembled slightly beneath his touch. Their gazes locked, and it was as though the room and everyone else in it apart from the two of them simply melted away.

'Dr Collins,' he heard himself intone gruffly, 'I am honoured to meet you.'

Only too aware that they were being observed, Zahir withdrew his hand and gestured towards the rectangle of Arabian couches positioned round a carved dark wood Moroccan coffee table a few feet away.

'We should sit and make ourselves comfortable. Jamal, you may serve coffee and refreshments now.'

'Of course, Your Highness.' The servant bowed and moved smoothly back towards the double doors, careful not to show his back to Zahir as he did so.

'Your rooms are comfortable and to your liking?' Moving his gaze from Jake Rivers to Gina, then back again to the man, Zahir settled himself on one of the longer couches and hoped the smile he'd arranged on his face was polite and relaxed—that it did not give rise to suspicion that he and Gina had met before and that the mere sight of her had all but undone him.

It was a most delicate predicament, and he would have to draw upon all his powers of diplomacy and tact to deal with it, he thought. But every time he found his glance returning to hers he wished they could be alone together, so that he could demand to know the real reason she had rejected him. *Had it been because there was someone else waiting for her back home in England?* How many times had he tortured himself with that thought over the years? *Too many.* One thing Zahir was certain of: before she left he would know *everything*...

'The palace is truly amazing, and our quarters more than comfortable—thank you,' Jake Rivers answered, linking his hands across his knees as he sat next to Gina. *How old was he?* Zahir wondered. He'd imagined that someone expert in their field, as he was supposed to be, would be older and more distinguished-looking. He could almost hear Farida teasing him. *That's because you watch too many old films where every English professor is a caricature,* she'd say. A sigh escaped him.

'That is good. As to the palace's origin, we believe it was erected in the ninth century, when the Persian and Byzantine wars were over. For the people of this region it has always been a powerful stronghold, and a symbol of strength to see off any foe. They have always helped maintain it, and take a pride in its beauty as well.'

Helplessly and hungrily, his gaze moved back to Gina. *What was she thinking?* he wondered. Was she shocked to learn his true identity at last? Would she curse her folly in turning him down? It was a bitter straw he would willingly grasp—a salve to his wounded pride that he'd never thought he'd receive.

'And your expertise is in antiquities, is it not, Dr Collins?' he asked. He saw her take a breath in and out again, then briefly fold her hands in her lap as if to compose herself.

'Classical antiquities and ancient artefacts… My colleague Dr Rivers is the historian in our team, Your Highness.'

'So you are equally qualified?'

'More or less.' Jake shrugged, throwing Gina an easy smile.

A stab of jealousy seared through Zahir's insides, his spine stiffening in protest at the envied familiarity. 'So Dr Collins is not your assistant?' he remarked, with a touch of mockery in his tone.

'My *assistant?*' Now the young man's lips split into a wide grin. 'I mean no disrespect, sir, but she is far too independent and bossy for that!'

'Is that so?' Zahir leant forward, his glance falling into a slow, leisurely examination of a pair of flawless china-blue eyes. 'How interesting…how interesting indeed…'

CHAPTER THREE

IF THEY had been with anyone but the Sheikh of Kabuyadir, Gina would have elbowed Jake in the ribs hard for his inappropriate teasing. He was developing into quite a brilliant historian, but he scored very few points for tact. Still, it really wasn't Jake at all who interested her in *this* discussion.

How could it be? It was the astounding discovery that it was *Zahir* who was 'His Highness'—handsome Sheikh of a historically once powerful Arabian kingdom and owner of the ancient and beautiful Heart of Courage. Never in her wildest dreams had she envisaged that that title belonged to *him*.

Why had he not told her the truth about who he was that night they'd spent together? And afterwards, when she'd returned home, he'd had ample opportunity to tell her when he phoned—but he hadn't. Had he feared that her decision to return would be swayed only by his exalted position and *not* the incredible man that he was?

'Dr Rivers and I are a team, Your Highness.' She blushed when she said his title, because it felt so surreal, yet her eyes hungrily cleaved to his strong tanned face and the long ebony hair that swung round his shoulders when he moved. He was dressed in traditional male clothing, and it was easy to see that the materials were much finer than anybody less privileged could afford. With his broad shoulders and natural air of command Zahir was every inch the esteemed ruler of his people, and seeing him again was like receiving a fresh supply of oxygen—as if for so long her ability to breathe freely had been compromised and Gina hadn't even known it.

'And we hope that our individual fields of expertise complement each other when it comes to undertaking our research,' she finished with a strained smile.

Making no immediate comment, Zahir continued to steadily hold her gaze. *Gina prayed that he couldn't see the longing, regret and dashed hopes reflected there.* Thankfully she heard the doors open behind her and guessed that Jamal had returned with their refreshments.

As he placed the large handmade brass tray down on the coffee table, the air was suddenly filled with the tantalising aroma of cardamom-spiced coffee. It was a delicacy that Gina had enjoyed when she was previously in Kabuyadir. Beside the small gold-rimmed cups, next to the coffee pot known as a *dallah,* on an ornate brass dish was an array of appetising-looking sweetmeats. One by one, Jamal served them their coffee. When he would have gone to Zahir first, his esteemed boss redirected him to Gina.

'We have lots to tell you about the Heart of Courage, Your Highness,' Jake piped up as Jamal bowed to Zahir, then discreetly left them to talk.

'Positive things, I presume?'

'Without a doubt… Its history is incredible. It's not every day that a historian is privileged enough to research an artefact that has its roots in the ancient Persian Empire.'

'So your own enquiry into its history has corroborated what I already know to be true about its origins? Then I am gratified that you welcomed the opportunity to research it. Were you similarly pleased, Dr Collins?'

'Of course… It's the chance of a lifetime for someone in my profession. The kind of thing we all dream of. To finally see the jewel for myself will be something I'll never forget, I'm sure.'

'Well, that will not be for a few days yet. You have both come a long way, and I would like you to relax and enjoy the hospitality of my palace first. The journey here was not too arduous for you?'

'Thanks to your kindness and generosity we travelled first class, Your Highness. I've never travelled in such luxury before. The trouble is, given the opportunity I'm afraid I could get used to it!' Jake answered, smiling.

'You have spent many weeks researching the jewel's history and provenance on my behalf, and you have travelled far to tell me what you have found. To make sure that you journeyed in comfort was the least I could do.'

'Once again, we thank you,' Gina said quietly.

A wave of heat submerged her when Zahir didn't seem to want to break his gaze from hers. *How was she supposed to bear this?* she wondered. How was she supposed to endure being so close to him when his high rank prohibited any possibility that they could enjoy a relationship again, even if they both desired it?

'Drink your coffee and take some refreshment, both of you. We will have plenty of time for our first discussion on the matter of the jewel tomorrow, after breakfast.'

When he turned his glance towards Gina again, Zahir's expression was hard to read. A wall had definitely descended, she intuited—a wall that had clearly been erected to prevent her from seeing too much.

'However, I am afraid I will not be able to join you for dinner tonight. There is a personal matter that takes me away from the palace for a while. I will direct Jamal to

show you to the dining room when it's time, and also show
you where to go for breakfast in the morning.'

She soaked in the deep Arabian bath, and scented herself
with the exotic oils supplied. A long, lazy bath was a pleasure Gina didn't allow herself very often. Where had she
learned the idea that she must *earn* the right to personal
pleasure? That work must come first? *Thinking of her parents, she didn't need to search hard for an answer.* But
blaming them wasn't to be considered—not when the way
she wanted to live was in her own hands now.

Sighing, she realised that she'd lingered in the warm
scented water a little too long. The water had started to
chill and goosebumps dotted her slim upper arms. She
stepped out onto the marble-tiled surround to dry herself
with a luxurious bathtowel that could have gone round her
slim frame twice. Dinner earlier had been impossible. All
she'd been able to do was watch Jake tuck into the feast that
had been prepared for them with gusto. How could she eat
when her stomach kept on roiling and lurching whenever
she thought of Zahir?

He'd left them in the salon alone to enjoy their coffee,
departing from the room without so much as a backward
glance. At dinner, sensing Jamal's hawk-eyed gaze on her
at every turn as she sat at the beechwood dining table inlaid
with exquisite mother-of-pearl, Gina had wrestled with
double misery at the idea her lack of appetite would cause
offence to the household in any way. She'd been utterly
relieved to finally escape to her room.

Wrapping herself in the generous white bathrobe she'd
found hanging behind the door, she moved back into the
bedroom, freeing her hair from its tidy French pleat to let
it tumble in buttery blonde waves down to her shoulders
as she went.

The knock on the door made her gasp. It was after midnight, and she could only surmise that it was perhaps a maidservant, wanting to find out what time she would be down for breakfast.

Drawing the edges of the voluminous robe together more securely, and tightening the belt, she drew back the door—only to be confronted by the tall, imposing figure of Zahir. In the corridor behind him all the lamps were turned down low, and the soft lighting created an even stronger warrior-like cast to his handsome features—particularly his eyes. They seemed to burn with the intensity of stoked flame as he stared down at her.

'My apologies for calling on you so late… As I told you earlier, something took me away from the palace for a while and I have only just returned.'

Clutching the sides of her robe tightly to her chest, Gina hardly knew what to think, never mind say. It didn't help that she was trembling from head to foot.

'May I step inside for a moment?'

Silently, she held the door wide, then closed it behind him. Glancing round the beautifully appointed room, Zahir sniffed the air and smiled. The gesture reminded her of the first time they had met in the Husseins' garden. The kindness she'd seen in his eyes then had prevented her from being afraid of him. But right now it wasn't kindness she saw reflected. There was an edge about him tonight that made her wary.

'You have been taking a bath?'

'I had no idea that you were Sheikh Kazeem Khan. It was such a shock to learn that it was you.' Her voice had a distinct quiver in it. 'I know it was three years ago, but I take it you haven't forgotten me?'

'Of course I haven't forgotten!' His glance was pained, his deep, resonant voice clearly irritated. 'Did you think I could ever forget that night? But to discover that the antiquities expert I hired in London is you is not exactly a delight to me… No, it is not. How could it be when you deceived me so callously?'

Twisting her hands in front of her robe, Gina felt like crying. 'Deceived you…how?'

'I fell in love with you that night…I thought you felt the same. I counted the days until you would return. You promised you would. When you told me on the phone that you had changed your mind, that returning was not realistic and you preferred to focus on your career, how do you think that made me feel? It was like a bomb exploding in my face!'

'It wasn't just because I wanted to focus on my career. My mother died unexpectedly just a couple of days after she was taken into hospital… I told you, remember? My father needed me to stay at home after that…to give him some support. We were both grieving…I hardly knew what I was doing. Kabuyadir seemed like a dream…'

Observing the harshness of Zahir's expression, Gina decided right then wasn't the time to tell him that her father had pleaded with her to stay in the UK and focus on her career in memory of her mother…told her that she shouldn't trust that life in Kabuyadir, living in a strange culture with a man she barely knew, could yield something better. Gina had buckled under the pressure of guilt and responsibility and agreed to stay, even when it had meant denying her desire to return to Zahir and the extraordinary passion they'd shared.

Now she was reeling at his confession that he'd fallen in love with her. There was a big part of her that could hardly believe such a handsome, charismatic man could truly have cared for her like that. To hear him say the words after all this time, compounding what a colossal mistake she'd made in not coming back to him, was like having her insides scraped raw with a sharpened blade.

'Whatever happened, clearly you thought my regard for you wasn't important enough to make you come back to Kabuyadir. Knowing that, I wonder that you have decided to return now three years later? If I had known that *you* were the antiquities expert I'd hired to research the jewel I would have taken steps to prevent your coming and hired someone else. My secretary Masoud would normally have acquainted me with such details, but he was suddenly taken ill and had to return to his family, otherwise I would have realised.'

'So…how are we to proceed from here on? Do you want me to act as though I never met you before?'

He abruptly turned away for a moment, as if to gather his thoughts. The sudden motion made the midnight-blue *jalabiya* he wore swirl round his leather-booted calves. 'What I want…what I wish…is that you had vanished off the face of the earth, if you want to know the truth! Then I wouldn't have to deal with the fact that you live and the possibility that you have chosen some other man to spend your life with rather than me.'

Gina gasped at the bitterness and passion she heard in his voice. 'There is no other man, Zahir…there never was. That's the truth.'

When he turned his gaze on her again his eyes regarded her with such disdain that she curled up inside. Somehow, no matter how hard she tried, she seemed to have great difficulty in inspiring love in the people closest to her.

'It is of no account to me any more. It is all too late now.'

Distressed and dry-mouthed at the bleakness in his tone, she darted out her tongue to moisten her lips. She wrapped her arms tightly round herself to subdue the pain that vibrated inside. 'Why didn't you tell me who you were?' she asked quietly. 'Have you any idea how hard it is for me to see you again and discover that you're practically a—a *king?*'

'I was not the ruler of Kabuyadir when we met. I knew I would inherit the mantle of Sheikh when my father died—I was trained to do so from a boy—but I was still just Zahir when we were together. I had thought to share some carefree time with you before that happened. When we met that night at the Husseins I, too, was grieving. My mother had died just a month before. To meet you and feel the way I did so instantly…it gave me hope—hope that life *would* get better despite my losing my beloved mother. However, you declined to come back to me. Just days after I spoke to you on the phone my father's health started to rapidly deteriorate, and he too died. Any prospect of carefree time had gone. I was now Sheikh of the kingdom and my life would never be the same again.'

Gina's heart contracted with sorrow at what Zahir had suffered. *No wonder her decision not to return had hit him like a hammer-blow.* 'So you've ruled this kingdom for three years? Did you marry?'

The taste of the question was bitter on her tongue, but Gina desperately needed to know the answer. She had kept her promise to her father and for the past three years had totally dedicated herself to work. There had been no other man in her life since that night with Zahir—she'd even acquired a reputation as 'uptight and frigid' with some of her less than gracious male colleagues. To think that Zahir might have married and relegated their precious time together to the far corners of his mind, rarely to be recalled or examined except maybe to remind himself of how deceitful she'd been in turning him down, stung worse than a thousand cuts.

'No. I did not.'

Her heart missed a beat. 'Why not?'

He folded his arms, immediately drawing Gina's hungry gaze to the impressive width of his chest. 'When it comes to marriage, a man in my position has a duty to marry for the utmost strategic and dynastic benefit. Believe it or not the neighbouring kingdoms are not exactly overflowing with available and eligible women. That is why I have not married yet.'

Falling silent for a moment, Gina couldn't help dwelling on one disturbing flaw in Zahir's reasoning. Lifting her troubled blue glance to his, she breathed in deeply. 'What about the Heart of Courage's prophecy? That the descendants of your family are destined to marry only for love?'

'What about it?' His tanned brow furrowed warningly.

When she'd discovered the story Gina had been utterly transfixed by it. It was so unbelievably romantic that she hadn't been able to help hoping that the jewel's current owner had also fulfilled the prophecy and fallen in love with a woman of his choice, instead of having to marry for convenience. Now she had learned that *Zahir* was the jewel's owner and custodian she felt as though she was caught in the eye of a fierce storm that would batter her to the ground, leaving her unable to rise to her feet ever again.

She swallowed hard. 'Doesn't it mean anything to you?'

'The jewel is a curse! For generations our family has fallen under the spell of that damned legend, which is why I want to finally be rid of it.'

Gina stared. '*That's* why you're selling it? Because you believe it's a curse?'

'The last people it cursed to a doomed marriage that ended in early death were my parents and my sister's husband Azhar. He was killed in a car accident just a few months ago. The toll of unhappiness and disaster just gets worse and worse, doesn't it? Now Farida goes about the palace like a wraith, hardly eating or sleeping, not engaging with anyone but me and the servants. Do you honestly think I would want to keep the jewel after that?'

'I'm really sorry that you and your sister have had to endure such terrible tragedy, Zahir.' Without realising it she used the name she knew him by, instead of his far grander title. 'But I'm sure you know that the jewel is priceless... *beyond* value. The whole world will be bidding for a chance to purchase it if you put it up for sale, and what about your own descendants? Your children and your sister's children, should she marry again? Won't you be depriving them of an important family heirloom, not to mention an artefact of peerless history and beauty?'

'Forgive me...but I thought I had merely hired you for your expertise in assessing the jewel's provenance? Not to give me your opinion about what I should and should *not* be doing with it!'

He strode to the door, his whole body bristling with formidable rage. If that rage could have been transmuted into matter, Gina would have seen dazzling sparks of flame shooting into the room, she was sure.

'I'm sorry...' Moving towards him, she felt distress deluge her. She could see he was in pain—both at the loss of his parents and at the disturbing way his beloved sister had withdrawn from the world—not to mention in shock upon seeing Gina again after she had rejected him. It made her yearn to be able to reach him, to comfort him in some way. 'If I've caused you offence...if I've hurt you by word or deed...I honestly regret it. Can you forgive me?'

With his palm curved round the gilt handle of the door, he stilled. The dark eyes grew even darker, but within their mesmerising reflection Gina saw a spark of haunting gold light.

'Forgiveness where you are concerned is not an easy matter. But I would ask that when you meet Farida, my sister, you do not mention the jewel under any circumstances. It would only distress her if she learns that I plan to be rid of it.'

'But what will I say if she asks me why I'm here?'

Zahir sighed. 'The palace is full of beautiful artefacts. You may tell her that you and your colleague are doing an inventory of the most valuable ones for me…as you did for Mrs Hussein's books.'

'I will do it because you ask me to, but I want you to know that I'm not comfortable with lying.'

To Gina's alarm, Zahir came closer. Her space was suddenly disturbingly invaded by the subtle but intoxicating scent of a cologne with hints of sandalwood and agarwood. She knew that particular essential oil was highly prized in the region.

Reaching out, he lightly curled his fingers round the tops of her arms. 'When I first saw you peeping out from behind the leaves of that jasmine I believed that you were a trusting innocent, incapable of deceit or subterfuge. To my bitter cost I have since learned that is not true. Apart from your undoubted beauty, Gina, there is nothing about you that could elicit my attention or regard again. You may as well tell me if there has been any other man in your life since we last met, seeing as it hardly matters to me now.'

'I told you the truth—there's been nobody else.' Her answer was as direct as the challenging look she gave him. 'And neither am I interested in another man. A relationship isn't my focus. I prefer to devote my time and attention to my work. Sometimes the paths it leads me down don't deliver exactly what I expect, but…unlike most men…it never disappoints me.'

Suddenly the grip on her arms grew tighter, and Gina bit back a gasp. 'When did I disappoint you? When I took you to bed? I have a photographic memory, *rohi*. I easily recall how incredibly responsive and eager you were in my arms that night. Yes, *eager*…even though you were untouched. Did you not think I'd realised that? Tell me, has there ever been another man in your life who has pleasured you longer or more ardently?'

Even though shock and embarrassment flooded her, she took heart at the distinct jealousy in Zahir's tone. He'd said she would never elicit his attention or regard again, but something in his possessive and furious manner told her that that might not be entirely true. Her senses clamoured and her pulses raced at the idea there might be a chance— even if that chance hung by the slimmest thread—that she could make things right between them.

Holding his hot and angry gaze, she breathed out slowly. 'You just told me you knew I was untouched when we went to bed…so the answer is no, Zahir. There has never been another man who has made me feel like you did that night.'

He abruptly released her. Dark eyes glittering, he silently surveyed her. 'For now, even though it is a hard thing for me to do, I will have to take your word on that. Tomorrow I will hear your presentation on the jewel, so please be well prepared. Goodnight, Dr Collins. I will see you in the morning.'

She stood frozen as he spun on his heel and exited the room, fervently wishing she had a magic spell to make him look at her fondly again instead of disparagingly…

* * *

Zahir's eyes burned from lack of sleep. When he had managed to doze a little, in his vast bed with its black silk sheets, he'd been tormented by only too real images of an alluring blonde angel with eyes bluer than a clear desert sky. He couldn't seem to get the scent of her out of his blood, either...

Frustrated beyond endurance, he dressed and went outside. In the sultry stillness of the perfumed night his footsteps led him to his own private garden—a sanctuary where the only other person allowed to enter was his gardener. Arriving at the Bedouin tent that was always kept ready for his use, Zahir took off his boots and unwound his broad leather belt. He laid a match to the dry tinder of the cooking fire and, sitting cross-legged before the flickering flames, placed the waiting coffee pot in the centre. As the tempting, comforting aroma of delicious Arabian coffee filled the night, Zahir rubbed the back of his hand across his tired eyes and stared out into the distance.

Apart from the crescent moon and its accompanying tapestry of bright stars the night was deep as an ocean and blacker than the wing of a raven... But he never at any time found it threatening. On many sleepless nights he had come out here to his private sanctuary and found that the enfolding darkness acted as a balm for the sorrow he'd endured daily since the death of his parents and since Farida had lost Azhar. *He'd also sought solace from the knifing hurt Gina had caused when she'd told him she wasn't returning.*

Stoking the fire a little with a stick, he watched the sparks crackle and spit, erupting into the air like tiny fireworks. *Gina...* He couldn't even erase her name from his mind, let alone her taunting image. Seeing her standing there in her bathrobe, all flushed skin and tousled golden hair, had been the most colossal temptation. He'd burned to hold her close again—so much so that his body had all but vibrated just because she was in the same vicinity.

For the past three years he had tormented himself almost beyond bearing that she was with another man. *Had she thought him a fool for trusting her so implicitly? For believing she would love him and only him for ever?* The thought had him gritting his teeth and clenching his jaw. Could anyone blame him for believing a part of her very being would always be his when it was to *him* that she'd given the gift of her innocence that night? It was true what he had told her—he *had* known she was a virgin. A fact that had made their instant passionate connection all the more sacred and special. At least that was what he'd thought then.

The Heart of Courage's taunting prophecy had not proved true in his case, Zahir reflected bitterly. *The sooner he was rid of that blasted jewel the better...* Before he started to believe its prophecy had some hold over *his* heart, too...

Reaching for the nearby folded checked cloth that lay in the sand, he wrapped it round the handle of the coffee pot and poured some of the rich aromatic brew into a waiting cup. Then, turning carefully, he crawled into the entrance of the large cloth tent and sat just inside, staring out at the fire's dancing kaleidoscope of flame as he thoughtfully sipped his drink.

Later—much later—he lay down on the silk cushions and woven rugs and slept a little. But not before seeing the spectacular rays of the dawn seep through the intricate weave of the dwelling's fabric-made walls...

Jake and Gina were having their breakfast on a canopied covered mosaic terrace. In the distance the sound of someone playing the *oud*—a stringed instrument that produced a haunting sound not unlike a Spanish guitar—floated hypnotically on the air.

The two colleagues were not alone. Jamal appeared at regular intervals, issuing curt instructions to two young housemaids to frequently hand round dishes piled high with fresh chunks of *khubuz*—the local bread—earthenware bowls of fat glistening black and green olives and dishes of *labneh*—a strained cream cheese that resembled yoghurt.

At the same time as Gina carefully opened the stopper on a slim bottle of olive oil, to drizzle it on her bread, she sensed a warm bead of perspiration sluggishly meander down her back. The sun was already high and hot in the azure sky, and the thin full-length yellow and gold kaftan she was wearing felt more like a winter coat beneath such unforgiving heat. She hadn't been able to resist sitting outside—not after enduring one of the longest and bitterest winters back home—but she was far from at ease. How could she be at ease after the way Zahir had left her last night?

He'd been so accusing and angry...a million miles away from the tender, beguiling man who had so easily swept her off her feet at first sight. Again, her heart ached to make things right between them, but how?

Adjusting her sunglasses, she watched Jake lift a generous chunk of bread that he'd liberally covered in slices of cucumber and wedges of dazzling red tomato to his lips and take a large bite. When he'd chewed and swallowed the food, Gina smiled. 'You've certainly got a healthy appetite.'

'That's true. But then I need to eat a lot to keep the old grey cells replenished!' he joked, grinning back at her.

This morning he was dressed in a wildly patterned Hawaiian-style loose shirt, which probably wouldn't have looked out of place on the beaches of Majorca or Corfu, and it definitely made him look eccentric. All he needed to top the outfit off was a knotted folded handkerchief on his head.

'Are you ready to present your notes on the jewel to His Highness?' he asked her.

'Ready as I'll ever be.'

Gina's mouth tightened. Just the thought of sitting in front of Zahir to discuss that amazing jewel with its heart-rending prophecy was akin to the prospect of walking across a bed of hot coals. She'd never been so nervous or so mentally under siege. Perhaps she shouldn't take it so personally that he now scorned the legend of marrying for love, but God help her she *did*.

After absenting himself for a while, Jamal reappeared on the terrace. 'After breakfast you are both summoned to see His Highness. I will wait here to escort you.'

Nervously scanning the food that yet again she'd barely touched, Gina met the far-seeing gaze of Zahir's personal servant and forced a scant smile as her insides churned and apprehension dried her mouth. 'Thank you.'

With a polite bow, and his hands behind his back, Jamal moved away to stand by the wall and wait.

CHAPTER FOUR

THE Sheikh of Kabuyadir's office was enormous—almost like a small ballroom, with its marble floor and exotic octagonal brass lamps with little coloured windows hanging down from the rafters of the high ceiling. A desk was definitely present. How could they ignore the six-foot-long burnished table that stood in the centre, with carved and cushioned antique chairs surrounding it? But Gina's eye was immediately drawn to the circle of colourful patterned cushions round a hand-woven blue, red and gold rug, to the right of the impressive desk, where Zahir sat, chin in his hands, crossed-legged and thoughtful.

He wore another broad leather belt round his long hooded black robe, and this one had an attachment that crossed over his chest and shoulder. It looked as if it might have accommodated a hunting knife or scimitar at some point, but right then the slim holster was empty. The image of Zahir as a brave ancient warrior was never far away, it seemed—*at least to Gina*. For three long years his striking visage had fuelled her fantasies and stoked her longing for him to an inferno at times—especially when she reflected on what she had lost by letting him go.

As they approached Jake gave a respectful nod, and under Jamal's hawk-like stare Gina did the same.

'You have breakfasted well, I trust?' Zahir's questioning

dark gaze encompassed both of them, but definitely lingered longer on her.

'Very well indeed, thank you.' This from an enthusiastic Jake.

'That is a nice shirt, Dr Rivers. Very…shall we say *colourful?*'

'I'm glad that you like it, Your Highness.'

'Sit down, please. We should make a start on the matter of the jewel.' Sweeping an extravagant hand round the circle of floor cushions, Zahir was suddenly all business.

His lightly mocking comment about Jake's shirt woke Gina to the unsettling fact that he had a sense of humour. Seating herself on the cushion the furthest in distance from their host, she spied a gleam which might have been amusement in the depths of his hypnotically brown eyes. It made her self-conscious and uncomfortable as she opened the slim leather document holder on her lap and carefully withdrew her notes. A couple of feet away from her, Jake did the same.

'I will start with you, Dr Rivers, if I may? Tell me what your historical research says about the jewel.'

Jake's enthusiastic report was followed by some intense discussion between the two men. Gina took the opportunity to observe Zahir at her leisure—starting with his voice. It was undoubtedly strong, yet he kept it modulated, varying the tone from time to time as his gaze focused unwaveringly on her colleague, and managing to give not the slightest indication of his private thoughts about what was being discussed at any time.

Now and again Jake shifted a little nervously—as if overwhelmed by where he was and who was quizzing him—but by and large he gave a good account of his painstaking research, and as the discussion ended, the merest smile touched the edges of Zahir's well-cut lips. At least he *appeared* pleased with what he had heard.

Then it was Gina's turn.

As Zahir directed his glance back to her, she had the panicked idea that his eyes were like the high-power lens of a high-resolution microscope, illuminating a specimen on a slide for detailed examination. *Right now she was the specimen.*

Fumbling with her papers as she cleared her throat to speak, she saw a few of the A-4 sheets slide off her lap and onto the patterned rug. She was mortified. Not exactly the best start, she thought, as she hurriedly gathered the papers and tidied them.

'Are you ready to proceed with your presentation now, Dr Collins?'

Hearing the sardonic edge to his tone didn't exactly help Gina's case. 'Yes, Your Highness.'

She made herself look him straight in the eye to give herself courage. After all, she was an expert in her field— not some nervous schoolgirl making a presentation for a class project.

'I thought I would start by discussing the fascinating legend that has grown up around the Heart of Courage.'

Where had that come from? It wasn't the first thing she'd intended discussing at all! The papers had got mixed up when they'd slid off her lap, and the sheet that had been at the bottom of the pile was now somehow on top. There was a sudden drop in temperature in the sultry air. Gina's glance collided with Zahir's. It was the iciest look she'd ever received. For a couple of excruciating seconds her breath was strangled inside her throat.

'I think not, if you don't mind, Dr Collins? I prefer to stick to verifiable facts right now. Speculation about any kind of mythical legend can only detract from a more

important discussion about the authenticity and provenance
of the jewel's origins. So we will stay with what is important
and not go off on some insignificant tangent…agreed?'

After such an unprepossessing beginning, Gina felt she
made a hash of the rest of her presentation. By the time it
came to an end, and Jamal had appeared with a tray of the
delicious cardamom-scented coffee for their refreshment,
she just wanted to flee back to her quarters and liberally
splash her burning face with ice water.

'Dr Collins? May I have a private word with you?'
Soundlessly, Zahir had materialised at her side, and was
holding out his hand to help her up from the floor cushion.
As she automatically slipped her hand into his, he turned
briefly to Jake. 'Dr Rivers, you should take your coffee
outside on the terrace and relax for a while. Later, Jamal
will give you a proper tour of the palace.'

'Thank you, Your Highness. I'll very much look forward
to that.'

When the twin doors had closed behind Jamal and Jake,
Zahir put his hands behind his formidable back and paced
the floor a little before turning back to Gina. There was
no mistaking the anger that transformed his breathtakingly
handsome features into an intimidating mask.

'What did you think you were doing, trying to make a
fool of me like that?'

'What do you mean?'

'Bringing up the legend…that's what I mean!'

'I—I had no intention of trying to make you look a fool.
I just got my notes muddled up and—'

His face was suddenly bare inches from hers, and the
sensation of her blood roaring in her ears blotted out any
others.

'Why should the tale of that cursed legend even be

amongst your notes when I have already told you I will have none of it?'

Hearts pounded a lot in romance novels, and now Gina knew *why*. She released the painful breath she'd been holding and nervously smoothed her hand down the side of her dress. 'In my search to establish the truth about an artefact I would hardly ignore anything that came up time and time again in the research—however unimportant or inconvenient a client regards it to be. My father taught me to fearlessly examine everything.' She unconsciously jutted her chin.

The man in front of her sighed heavily and rubbed his forehead. 'Your father?'

'He's a professor of antiquities and ancient history back home.'

'Ah, yes… The man you deemed more important than coming back to me.'

'He's my only remaining family,' Gina said miserably. 'He needed my support.'

Zahir's hot temper dissipated as abruptly as sometimes a sandstorm in the desert came to an end. How was a man with healthy red blood coursing through his veins supposed to ignore the tempting vision before him and resist? Especially when the vision was all glittering blue eyes, flushed cheeks and quivering coral-glazed lips—the lower slightly fuller than the upper, and so divinely shaped that they would drive a sane man *mad?*

'When it comes to his work he's very diligent and—and…' the big blue eyes were staring at him as though transfixed '…thorough. He doesn't leave any stone unturned.'

The space between them seemed to thrum with electricity.

'Is that so?' Zahir responded softly.

Before Gina had a chance to answer him, his mouth

claimed hers. His possession was clumsy and rough at first, because of his desperation to taste her again, but then he pulled her to him, and her slim body sagged against his, so that he felt every undulating curve and dip, and he kissed her more slowly and seductively. Kissed her and sampled her intoxicatingly addictive flavours until the heat in his blood consumed him like an inferno—until he wished he had the power to make the rest of the world go away, simply to forget about affairs of state, and the threatening insurgence in a local mountain region that would command the rest of his day, and take her to bed. And when he got her in his bed he would ravish and pleasure her until she was quivering in his hands…until she wept and swore she wanted only him—that any other man she had ever known since they met was erased from her mind and heart for ever.

His hands were in her hair, his fingers massaging her scalp, when he finally raised his head to look down at her. Aware that he was breathing hard, he smiled unabashed. 'You taste even more delectable than I remember. I had not foreseen the end of our meeting finishing like this, Gina, but I suppose after what happened between us the first time we met it was inevitable.'

She tried to prise herself free from his arms, but Zahir was having none of it. Right then he didn't even care if Jamal or one of the other servants walked in and saw him. They had sworn their fealty to him at his coronation, and no tittle-tattle would leave the palace—he was certain of that.

'Let me go, please! We can't—we shouldn't—'

'There is nothing to fear. There will be no stain of dishonour on you should we be seen together, Gina. This is *my* palace, remember? I am the law-maker in this kingdom.'

'I'm not worried about what anyone else thinks if they

see us together, but I *am* concerned about how I conduct myself while I'm here. I came here for professional purposes only, to present the results of my research. I'm not here as a personal friend of yours. I'm also here with a colleague.'

'You are concerned about what the diminutive Dr Rivers with his tasteless loud shirts thinks?'

'He may not have your stature or standing, or indeed your *dress sense,* Zahir, but he is a good man—a man who might be hurt if he finds out I knew you from before and didn't tell him.'

He muttered a well-used Kabuyadir curse and released her abruptly. 'Why should he be hurt?' he demanded, his heart hammering wildly inside his chest. 'Are you telling me that you two are having an affair?'

Gina appeared slightly dazed by the question. 'Me and Jake…? No, of course not!'

'Then why should you care what he thinks?'

'Out of respect—nothing more.'

Owning to feeling thoroughly dissatisfied with her answer, Zahir gave her a distinctly cool glance before turning away and striding across to the large desk. Pulling open a hidden drawer, he retrieved a small ornate knife with a high-polished blade that was pointed at the end. He slid it into the previously empty leather sheath on his belt and once more swung round to face her.

'I have to go out, so our business is at an end for now.'

'Where are you going? And why do you need that weapon?'

'There's a band of lawless rebels in the mountains who have been visiting local villages at night and causing trouble. They have received warnings from my council before, but still they continue to make a nuisance of themselves. Now I need to go and address them personally.'

Gina walked towards him a few steps, her expression alarmed. 'Isn't that dangerous? You're not going there alone?'

Liking the feeling that she cared about whether or not he might get hurt, Zahir allowed himself a lazy smile. 'I am not Zorro, Gina. I will of course be accompanied by a small detachment of trained soldiers.'

'But still…' She twisted her hands in front of the gold and yellow kaftan that so fluidly fell to her feet, caressing her shapely but svelte body underneath on its way. 'Please be careful.'

'I have too much at stake here to take unnecessary risks… My beloved sister, for one.' Aware that he sounded aloof and distant, and that he'd made a point of telling Gina it was his sister he cared most about in the world above anyone else, Zahir knew he was feeling anything *but* aloof towards the lovely woman who stood in front of him. Whenever he was near her molten heat seemed to beat an urgent path to his loins, and now was no exception.

'Of course.' She dipped her head.

'Later, when I return,' he continued, 'there is another matter that I would very much like to discuss with you. Even if it is late you should make yourself available. Do you understand?'

The prettily shaped chin that he could cup in one hand if he had a mind to jutted forward in surprise. The big blue eyes sparkled defiantly. 'Is that some sort of royal command?'

Her rebellious stance stunned Zahir. *It also aroused him.* His hands itched to touch her, sweep her high into his arms and carry her to his private apartments to do with as he willed. Knowing he could not, because even now his detachment of soldiers awaited him in the courtyard, he promised himself that he would teach her the most exquisite lesson later...

'Yes,' he bellowed, then swept past her to the twin doors, 'it *is!*'

Feeling on edge and restless, knowing that Zahir might possibly be in danger and that there was nothing she could do about it, Gina made a poor effort at eating lunch that day. *At this rate she'd return home to England looking like a bag of bones!* But how was she supposed to eat when fear that she might never see him again all but made her crazy?

That incendiary kiss they'd shared earlier had irrevocably reminded her why he was the only man in the world she could ever love. The warm pressure of his mouth and the hot silken tongue that had passionately invaded her had left an indelible tingling imprint, and she longed to experience more of the same.

She decided to try to distract her mind by asking Jamal if she could explore the palace grounds a little on her own. He immediately offered to escort her, as he had done Jake earlier, but she persisted in her request to go unaccompanied. With obvious reluctance in his expressive amber eyes, he agreed.

There were several paved paths—some extravagantly shaded—meandering into the lush gardens. Birdsong abounded. Various enchanting scents hung in the air. Gina detected jasmine, orange blossom and heliotrope amongst others. Everywhere she glanced there were ornate fountains and stately stone statues—presumably of ancestors of the illustrious Kazeem Khan family? If her mind hadn't been so distracted with worry about Zahir, and if she'd known for certain that he was safe, Gina might have allowed herself to investigate the statues further, indulge her love of history and genealogy together and truly revel in the discoveries she made. But under the circumstances, that was easier said than done.

She was almost level with the slight, black-robed veiled figure sitting on a bench before she realised she should probably retrace her steps in case she was intruding on someone's peaceful contemplation. It was a woman—a young, elfin-faced woman—with the prettiest brown eyes and yet perhaps the saddest expression Gina had ever seen.

'Who are you?' the woman asked, first in her own language and then, when Gina didn't immediately respond, in English.

'I'm so sorry if I disturbed you. I'm Dr Gina Collins, and I'm here to help make an inventory of the palace artefacts for His Highness.' She bit her lip after this announcement, feeling more than just slightly guilty as she did as directed and supplied her alleged reason for being there.

'My brother did not tell me he intended to make such an inventory.'

'Forgive me…your *brother?*'

'I am Farida, and the Sheikh of Kabuyadir is my brother…although lately he is becoming more and more like a stranger to me.'

This was followed by a heavily troubled sigh. Standing stock still, Gina half expected to be waved away and told not to intrude on this particular part of the garden again. But to her surprise, Farida turned up her face and smiled.

'It is nice to see another young woman about the place—someone from England, too. Zahir and I both went to university there—did you know that?'

Feeling a jolt of surprise, Gina shook her head. 'I didn't. Where did you study?'

'We both went to Oxford—he to Pembroke College, to

study politics and economics, and me to Lady Margaret Hall to study English and modern languages.'

'You're clearly both very bright. I'm afraid my grades weren't good enough to get me to Oxford.'

'Zahir's mind is like a rapier. Mine is a little slower, but I get there eventually.'

'And you liked it at Oxford?'

'It is a fascinating city. Full of stunning architecture and history and learning and all the things I love—especially books. I was always the family bookworm. Whatever the time of day, I could usually be found with my head in some fascinating tome even before I went up to Oxford. But all that changed when I met Azhar...' Her words trailed off, her expression became subdued, and she was clearly lost in thought again.

Gina's heart squeezed tight as she remembered Zahir telling her that Farida's husband Azhar had died in a car accident. She was so young...*too* young to be a widow.

Before she'd realised her intention, she dropped down onto the bench beside her. 'Azhar was your husband?' she said gently.

Farida nodded sadly. 'He was the love of my life. I have been so lost since he died. I don't really know what to do with my life any more. I don't believe I have anything left to offer anyone—even the brother I have always adored. Everything just seems futile.'

'For a long time after he lost my mother, my father told me he felt like that, too. His method of coping with his grief was to lock himself away in the house and bury himself in his work. I didn't really know how strongly he felt about her until recently. Their marriage always seemed more of a pragmatic arrangement than anything else. I honestly thought that their relationship was more a meeting of minds than hearts. But lately—lately I've started to believe I was wrong about that.'

Farida's soft brown gaze studied Gina for a long time before she finally spoke. 'I believe that love is everything… that no relationship or marriage can survive for long without it.'

'And I believe that true love can never die. Wherever your beloved Azhar is now, he watches over you and only wants the best for you. I firmly believe that he would want you to enjoy the rest of your life and live it to the full, with his blessing.'

To Gina's surprise, the other woman laid her hand over hers. 'Thank you, Gina. I may call you that? You have said something very important to me that will help me sleep a little easier tonight. How long do you stay in Kabuyadir?'

She flushed a little. A buzzing insect flew by her ear and she brushed it away. 'I'm not sure. It depends how long the work I've been hired to do takes. I'm here with a colleague, by the way…Dr Rivers.'

'I hope it takes a long time.' Farida smiled. 'For I feel that I have just made a new friend.'

Unbearably touched, and because she feared the same debilitating grief would be visited on her should anything happen to Zahir, Gina found her blue eyes misting over for a second. 'The feeling is mutual…you're very kind.'

The loudly insistent tattoo beaten on her bedroom door that night woke Gina from an already far from serene sleep. She hadn't bothered undressing because Zahir had told her to make herself available to talk when he returned. Even though she'd resented the command at the time, now she prayed he'd live to shout another one.

Shoving off the exotic silk counterpane, she got hurriedly to her feet.

'Dr Collins—His Highness desires your presence in his chambers immediately!' Looking as if he'd run all the way through the palace to reach her, beneath his dark red fez Jamal's forehead was lightly coated with glistening sweat.

Light-headed with shock, Gina held on to the doorframe to anchor her for a moment. 'What's happened? Has he been hurt?'

'Come.' Jamal gestured impatiently. 'No questions. Please come now.'

Not bothering to turn back and put on the pretty sequinned slippers she'd left by the bed, she pulled the door to and followed Zahir's officious servant down the marble corridor barefoot.

CHAPTER FIVE

BARELY registering the vast bedroom she was shown into, Gina's focus was on the strongly built man whose long dark hair was spread out against a bank of plump pillows on the emperor-size bed where he lay. His impressive bronzed chest was bare apart from the stark white bandage encircling his ribcage. A spectacled man with a neat black beard, she could only assume was the court physician, attended him. She bit back a gasp when she saw the spreading red stain beneath another neatly applied bandage round his hard-muscled bicep. The physician was just withdrawing a hypodermic needle from Zahir's uninjured arm, and both men glanced round immediately as Jamal opened the door and ushered her inside.

'Dr Collins...you have me at rather a disadvantage, I am afraid. Come closer. I won't bite you. I hardly have either the energy or the strength for that right now!'

How could he joke at a time like this? Gina thought as she hurried forward towards the bed. 'You're hurt. What happened?'

'Some foolish rebel leader thought he'd make a name for himself by killing the ruler of Kabuyadir—that's what happened! Luckily his ill-timed bullet only glanced against my arm and side. Do not look so worried, Dr Collins...my doctor has already assured me I'm going to live.'

Again the jokey manner. She could hardly understand it. Did he really take the fact he'd almost been killed so lightly? 'That's not funny. Don't you have a bodyguard or someone looking out for you when you do this kind of thing?' Because she was worried and upset, it was hard to control the quaver in her voice.

'My bodyguard took a bullet in the leg and is now being taken care of in hospital.'

Zahir's voice was full of frustration, and for a moment she saw regret and anger in his glance. She suddenly wished that Jamal and the doctor would leave them alone together, so that she could ascertain for herself how he was really feeling. Something told her he must be putting on a front of some kind. But then his rich dark gaze turned surprisingly warm as he surveyed her. To add to her surprise, he reached for her hand and possessively held it—clearly unconcerned that his physician and servant bore witness to the gesture.

They watched in silence as the doctor collected the tools of his trade and returned them to a bulky leather case. He spoke briefly in their shared language to Zahir, and his patient nodded as he listened. Then the man respectfully bowed, before backing away towards the door. Jamal held it open for him.

Catching his servant's eyes, Zahir said in English, 'You may leave us. I will be perfectly all right now. Shortly I will take the good doctor's advice and get some sleep. Make sure news of the incident does not reach my sister's ears before I get the chance to tell her myself.'

'Yes, Your Highness.'

The door quietly closed, leaving them alone.

Staring down at the small slender hand he still clasped in his, Zahir raised it to his lips and planted a tender kiss there.

Biting her lip, Gina felt tears spring to her eyes. 'You shouldn't take such terrible risks,' she murmured, and she didn't care that he was a ruler of a kingdom. To her he was just a man—a man whose welfare she cared about more than any words could possibly convey.

'I do not like this—that I make you weep,' he said gently, brushing away the damp trail that wet her cheek. 'And trust me—this is *not* how I'd planned to spend the night with you.'

She did a mental double-take as his provocative words registered. Tugging her hand free from his clasp, she stared. 'Spend the night? What are you talking about, Zahir?'

'Do you *really* not understand me?'

'I told you already that I am here in a professional capacity only—that I—' She couldn't continue, because sudden self-consciousness had robbed her of the power to keep talking. The man lying atop the great bed, in black silk pyjama bottoms that fastened at least an inch and a half beneath his belly button, clearly did not share her problem. Tearing her gaze away from his perfectly taut stomach and slim bronzed hips, she found her body flooded with disconcerting heat.

His sculpted lips curved in the most licentious smile. 'You can assume your professional capacity—whatever that means—during the day, but what is to stop us being together during the night? I know you are not immune to my attentions, even though you might hide behind the cover of your professional role.'

'Look…I know you're hurt, and you're probably just looking for some kind of comfort, but I'm not jumping into bed with you just because—because it happened before.' *If you could honestly forgive me for my mistake in not coming back,* Gina thought anguished. *If you really believed in the love I thought we shared that night we were together…*

then nothing could stop me sharing your bed. But I know because of what you now feel about the Heart of Courage's prophecy—and because you think I rejected you without a single regret—that that's not the case.

'I have a proposition for you.' His dark-eyed glance didn't waver. 'That's what I wanted to see you about.'

'And that is?'

'I am not going to waste time play acting and pretending I don't desire you, so I will get straight to the point. Many wealthy and powerful men in my position take a mistress. I haven't done so yet because I have never met a woman to meet all my requirements in every way. That is not until you came into my life again, Gina. I would like you to stay here in Kabuyadir. If you stayed you would not want for anything…*ever*. Anything you wanted that it was within my power to give you, you would have.'

She didn't know whether to laugh or cry. Beneath her robe her heart thudded painfully. Moving away from the side of the bed, she tucked a loose tendril of shining blonde hair back. 'I gather I'm meant to take such an offer as a compliment?'

'At least it shows I am not rejecting you as you so easily rejected me. At least I am being honest about the fact that I want you in my bed again.'

'Lust is a poor substitute for genuinely caring about someone, Zahir.' She wouldn't say the word 'love' in his presence…not yet. Not while he was clearly intent on some-how making her pay for not returning to him three years ago. Still she would not close the distance between them, and a soft sigh escaped her. 'Do you think I should settle for that because you feel I owe you in some way? Anyway, I can't stay here indefinitely. Once I've given you all the information I have on the jewel—and seen it for myself—I'll be heading home again. I have a job to get back to—a job that I've wanted for a long time and worked hard to get. I also have a father who hasn't been very well lately, so I'm afraid you'll just have to find someone else to fill the position of Sheikh's mistress.' She started to walk across the marble-tiled floor towards the door.

'Gina!'

His call stopped her in her tracks. Alarmed, she turned to see that Zahir had moved to the edge of the bed and was getting to his feet. She saw him sway a little, and dashed back to his side.

'What do you think you're doing? For goodness' sake, get back to bed before you do some irreparable damage to yourself!'

'What do *you* care?' he retorted sulkily, reluctantly allowing her to help him lie down and rest his head against the stack of plump pillows again. 'You would leave on the first plane home without caring whether I lived or died.'

'Don't be ridiculous.'

'You sound just like an old spinster teacher of mine. Of course you don't look like her in any way. Do you know what torment it is to me to have you so close, to smell your perfume and not be able to touch you the way I long to? It is a double agony for *this* to have happened to me today. Now not only am I sexually frustrated but I'm in physical pain from a blasted bullet wound, too! It will take more than a strong sleeping pill to make me sleep tonight.'

The strong bronzed brow crumpled a little in obvious pain, and Gina tenderly pushed back the hair from his smooth unlined forehead and frowned. 'Why did you have to go and deal with this trouble yourself? I wish you'd sent someone else instead—the captain of your army perhaps? Someone used to dealing with these volatile situations?'

'You think I am incapable of dealing with a physical threat from a few hot-headed rebels?'

'I'm not questioning your ability for combat, Zahir. You certainly look intimidating and strong enough. But it seems like a reckless thing to have done when you didn't have to.'

He tensed and gave her a fierce glare. 'And how would *you* know what I do and don't need to do? I am not just some useless figurehead or cardboard cut-out prince who sits in the palace issuing orders. I am a politician and diplomat, too, and after many months of this rebel faction employing their bullying tactics on peaceful villages it was time to step in and demonstrate once and for all that my kingdom is not going to simply sit back and accept it! Who better to bring that message home to them but the ruler himself?'

'Please don't get so worked up. I'm afraid you'll re-open your wounds if you get too upset.'

'You can go now.'

'What?' Taken aback by the curt dismissal, Gina froze.

'You are both a painful distraction and an annoyance, and what I need right now is some peace and quiet to contemplate the situation and recover.'

'All right, then. I understand.'

Just as she made to leave Zahir reached for her, curving his big hand round the back of her neck to pull her face down to his. His angry kiss was hot, hard and passionate, with no pretence at being anything other than punishing.

Gina stumbled, her tongue flicking to the stinging spot on her lower lip when he suddenly released her.

'Now you can go.'

His glittering dark-eyed glance made her limbs feel heavy as lead. Reaching the door, she exited the sumptuous room hardly knowing how she managed it...

* * *

A wounded bear was said to be dangerous. The following morning, walking alone in his private garden, Zahir felt his wounds throbbing and painful, and reflected on the crazy rebel who had inflicted them on him and his bodyguard. He was hurt, angry, and liable to lash out verbally at anyone who dared to come near.

Thankfully his servant Jamal intuited his moods well. The man's patience and understanding seemed to silently embrace even the most unpredictable and sombre shades of his employer's personality. Earlier he had brought Zahir coffee. Thinking of Gina—and how he had treated her last night—he had irrationally flung the small brass tray across the courtyard. Everything had landed in the previously calm waters of the ornamental pond, but Jamal had immediately hurried to retrieve it all and clean up the mess without batting an eyelid.

In an hour's time, after he had been examined again by his physician, Zahir was due to address a meeting of his council regarding the uprising by the rebels. But right now the topic that consumed him even more than that was definitely *Gina.* He had offered her a situation that most women would have grabbed at—but, no. Not *her.* Instead she preferred to put her job and her ailing father back at home before him…*again!*

While he privately had a grudging admiration for her loyalty to both her job and her family, it didn't stop him from feeling intensely jealous and aggrieved that he still clearly featured so low on her list of priorities. But he could not let her leave so easily. He had to find a way of making her stay in Kabuyadir for longer than just a few short days. After seeing her again he knew he would not easily get her out of his blood a second time—no matter *how* angry he was.

'Zahir!'

A slight, dark-robed figure was hurrying towards him along the paved pathway, arms extended. As his sister reached him, she all but stole the breath from his lungs when she threw herself into his arms. Zahir couldn't stop the grunt of pain he emitted as her body collided with the inflamed bandaged wound at the side of his ribcage.

As she stepped back in alarm, he saw the damp smudges beneath Farida's pretty eyes—evidence that she'd already been weeping.

'I couldn't believe it when I heard that you'd been shot. Why didn't somebody tell me? Was it because you ordered them not to? I'm not some little child you have to constantly protect, you know. I was a married woman until recently, and I won't fall apart if I hear bad news—even if it frightens me. What on earth possessed you to travel into the heart of the brigands' stronghold with just a handful of soldiers and a bodyguard?'

Zahir could hardly believe his ears. Here was another woman chastising him for doing his utmost to resolve a situation that was bringing fear and suffering to his people! Had his *father's* actions been questioned with such doubt and disbelief? He didn't think so.

The scowl on his face was inevitable. 'I had to try and talk to their leader. He's a hot-headed egomaniac, seeking to gain power by getting a band of similar unthinking idiots to rob and intimidate the villagers. In the end—when I saw that reason simply did not compute with him—I gave him a warning that if there was any more trouble I would imprison the lot of them for life. We were just about to make our return home when he pulled out a pistol and started firing.'

'You could have been killed!'

'Yes, but I wasn't.' He rubbed a weary hand across his eyes. 'Please do not fear for my safety so much, little sister.

I would hate to think that you were fretting every time I set foot outside the palace walls!'

'But somebody *shot* you, Zahir. Do your wounds hurt badly?'

Seeing the loving concern on her dear face, Zahir retrieved his sense of humour. 'Not badly. They're *inconvenient,* more than anything.'

'What do you mean?'

A stirring image of Gina fleshed out nicely in his mind—one in which she was wearing only her bathrobe, her golden hair all mussed and sexy, her cheeks flushed from a steamy bath and the scent of exotic oils clinging to her exquisitely soft skin. Straight away the thought acted as a flaming torch, igniting his blood.

His ensuing smile was almost painful. 'I only mean that I will probably not be as active as I would like for the next few days.'

'What about the man who shot you? What happened to him?'

'Right now he is languishing in a prison cell in the city. He was taken there last night by my guards.'

Farida patted down the silk *hijab* that covered her hair, neck and shoulders, and looked perturbed. 'There is no chance that one of his men will try and seek revenge and hurt you again, Zahir?'

'If they dare, my punishment will ensure they will never pick up a firearm or a weapon again. Not in this lifetime!'

But even as he contemplated such a repugnant reality, a wave of doubt and concern rolled through him. *Had he made a huge error in judgement, thinking that he could reason with such a lawless band?* Now wasn't the time to consider such a disturbing notion—not when Farida was so clearly worried and upset.

He laid his arm reassuringly round his sister's slender shoulders. 'The palace is a steadfast fortress that has stood the test of time. No amateur trigger-happy fool is going to get at me here. They would be crazy to even try. Now, enough talk about that. Let us discuss more pleasant things, hmm? What are you planning on doing with yourself this day?'

They were walking back along the shaded pathway, and the balmy agarwood scented air seemed to ease Zahir's troubled mind with its rich and mysterious fragrance as they walked.

'I hope to spend some time with Gina Collins, actually.'

'You have met Dr Collins?' Stopping dead in his tracks, Zahir stared at his sister in surprise.

'Yes, I have met her, and I like her very much. She said something rather wonderful to me about Azhar that gave me great comfort. I don't have many girlfriends around my own age, so it's very nice to have someone like Gina staying at the palace for a while. As you have employed her to make an inventory of some of the more important family artefacts, I thought I might be able to assist her? What do you think?'

The little speech she had just made was so surprising, so unexpected, that it took Zahir a few moments to digest it properly. It was the first time since Farida had been so tragically widowed that she'd shown even the slightest interest in anything other than her own misery. If Gina had been able to effect such a dramatic change—even in the short time she'd been here—what else might her presence be able to achieve? Zahir's mind raced with something that felt very much like hope.

'I am sure that if I speak with her on your behalf she

would be only too happy to have your help. Do you by any chance know where she is now?'

'I was just about to go and look for her.'

'Let me do that. Why don't you stay out here for a little while in the shade and relax? When I've discussed your suggestion with Dr Collins I will send Jamal to come and fetch you, okay?'

'She is very pretty, brother…don't you think?'

She is beautiful beyond imagining, his mind answered immediately. But Zahir curbed the words that hovered on his tongue for something a little more measured. After all, he didn't think it wise to alert Farida to his deepening interest in Gina—or the fact that he had asked her to become his mistress!

'Yes.' He allowed the briefest smile to touch his lips. 'She is very pretty…clever, too.'

He turned away before he had the urge to elaborate further on all Gina Collins's very appealing attributes…

On returning to her luxurious rooms the previous night, Gina had known that sleep would elude her for the rest of the night-time hours. After her encounter with the man who set her heart racing like no other, finding him injured and then *furious* when she refused his offer to become his mistress, she'd been both distressed and heartbroken. It shocked her that he had such apparent disregard for his own safety—so much so that he would venture into a lawless region of his kingdom to deal with some gun-toting rebels. Did he not realise how much the people close to him cared for him?

But she was hurt, too, because all he seemed to be interested in as far as she was concerned was appeasing his lust. Had she imagined the tender words and fervent feelings he'd declared when they'd first encountered each other in the Husseins' garden? Then she'd been so sure of his mutual love and affection that she'd given him her most precious gift. Had that meant *nothing* to him?

At breakfast out on the terrace, she ate very little. Her obvious lack of appetite even prompted Jake to comment.

'Are you feeling all right, Gina? You've got dark circles under your eyes and you've barely touched your food.'

'I'm fine,' she murmured. 'Just a little tired.'

'The heat can do that. Best take things easy today,' her companion responded consolingly.

Beckoning Jamal over to the table, after Jake had returned to his rooms to locate a book, Gina nervously enquired about Zahir's condition. The taciturn servant told her that His Highness was 'comfortable' and back on his feet, but she should be prepared for the possibility that she might not see him at all that day. His physician had told him that he must rest.

She then politely asked if she could use the palace library. Informing her that he was instructed that she and her colleague Dr Rivers should be aided wherever possible to undertake their work, he agreed. If the man had any thoughts about why the Sheikh should have summoned her last night to his private rooms when he had just been injured, neither by word nor deed did he give them away.

A library had always represented a comforting safe place to Gina. Often, during her childhood, she had taken refuge there when life had felt hard and there hadn't seemed to be a lot of love or affection going round. Books were her friends—constant loving companions that didn't let her down.

Zahir's library took her breath away. It was a repository for the written word that only the richest and most devoted imagination could conjure up. Shelf upon shelf of books ancient and modern confronted her, practically reaching up to the sky. Amid the shelves of books were sumptuous couches and chairs in which a browser could relax and peruse the book they'd selected. The ambience was not unlike that of a breathtaking cathedral, with a high-vaulted ceiling made of sandstone and granite interspersed with mosaic.

Gina had a plan. She was going to try and delve more deeply into Zahir's family, going right back through as many generations as possible. There must be hundreds of history books on the region here, chronicling the dynasty through the centuries. If luck was on her side she might even come across old family journals...*they* would be her primary sources. She wanted to discover as much extra information as she could on the family's association with the famed Heart of Courage, but she had to be discreet. If Zahir found out what she was doing he could very well put her on the next plane home and forbid her from visiting Kabuyadir again...

'There you are'

Immersed in the pages of a fascinating book she'd pulled from a shelf, Gina spun round in shock at the sound of Zahir's voice. He was as imposing as usual, in his dark robes and broad leather belt, his ebony hair like a velvety dark river rippling down over his shoulders. Straight away she noticed there was a light sheen of sweat on his brow, and she realised he must be in pain.

'What are you doing up and about? Shouldn't you be resting after what happened?' Anxiously she clutched the dusty volume she'd been examining to her chest. A ray of sunlight beamed in through the cathedral-like narrow windows and warmed her back.

'I've been walking in the garden, getting some air. I cannot stay confined to my bed for twenty-four hours a day just because I took a couple of small flesh wounds. Jamal told me I would find you here. What do you think of my library?'

'It's truly magnificent. A person could spend a lifetime in here and barely get through the books on even *one* shelf.'

Her comment drew the hint of a smile to his lips. Moving towards her, he moved his hand briefly to his side.

'Are you hurting?' she asked. The distressed catch in her voice sounded loud to her own ears.

'That question is a double-edged sword. The truth is that my pride is stinging just as much as my physical wounds.'

'Why's that?'

'I...' He seemed to swiftly reconsider what he'd been going to say and lightly jerked his head towards the book Gina pressed to the white silk of her blouse. 'What have you got there?'

'It's a history of the Byzantine empire.' She sent up a silent prayer of thanks that he hadn't discovered her with an incriminating family journal, but she still couldn't help colouring guiltily.

'A little light reading, eh?' he joked, brown eyes twinkling.

Her insides melted like butter over a hot stove. Staring back at him, she fell into a hypnotic semi-trance.

'I am sorry I treated you as I did last night,' he murmured, 'my behaviour was reprehensible.'

Now he was tipping up Gina's chin, gazing at her as though he, too, was hypnotised.

'You were hurt and angry... I understand, Zahir. I understand and I forgive you. But right now you clearly should be resting—not up and about like this, putting a strain on your wounds.'

She held her breath as his fingers moved across her cheek and into her hair. 'Could any man blame me for wanting you so much?' he said, and his usually strong voice sounded distinctly unsteady.

CHAPTER SIX

THE spell he cast was so profound, so intense, it was as if the rest of the world suddenly ceased to exist. There were no boundaries or walls any more—just Zahir and her, suspended in a weightless loving universe where who you were and the roles you assumed in life—whether antiquities expert or sheikh—ceased to matter. All there was were two souls recognising each other and silently rejoicing.

Her eyelids drifted closed as every cell vibrated with anticipation, waiting for the kiss that was bound to come.

It felt as though everything in his life had been teetering on the brink of disaster for a long time. Now, studying the entrancing beautiful features before him, Zahir thought that here was one thing that was right...that made him feel good...after talking to his sister *even* hopeful.

From his head to his feet his body yearned for this woman. He could scarcely think of anything else but losing himself inside her. His longing overrode even the unholy biting sting of his gunshot wounds. *And then he saw it...* A slightly raised scarlet abrasion on the plump pink flesh of her lower lip. Her mouth was naked this morning— free from make-up—so it was plain to see. Instantly he recoiled—the memory of the savage kiss that had been his parting shot last night dousing the heat that enveloped him like ice-water.

'I did this?' He winced as he stroked the pad of his thumb over the lightly swollen wound.

The incandescent long-lashed eyes appeared startled. Realising what he meant, she coiled her slender fingers gently round his wrist. 'You didn't mean to.' Her tone was warm and whisper-soft. 'It's nothing to be concerned about.'

'I meant to make you pay for my frustration, and that is not the action of a man who is honourable. A thousand apologies, Dr Collins…it will not happen again.'

He made himself withdraw in every way—physically, psychologically, mentally. It was agony, but Zahir had to do it.

Her face was a picture of confusion. 'It's nothing to feel guilty about. It happened in the heat of the moment.'

'Even so…' Inside, he was thinking, *I do not deserve her forgiveness. I acted like an arrogant fool.* 'The reason I came to find you,' he continued, 'is to ask something of you that will mean a lot to me.'

'Tell me.'

'My sister Farida informs me that you have already bumped into each other. It appears she has taken a great liking to you. It's the first time she has shown an interest in anyone or anything outside of the palace since she lost Azhar, so naturally I want to encourage it. She wants me to ask if she can help you with your inventory of some of the more important palace artefacts. I know I have not officially asked you to undertake such a project, but I am asking you now. Will you do it? Both conduct an inventory and allow Farida to assist you?'

She stroked her palm down over her hip in the pearl-coloured silk harem pants she'd matched with a tunic in the same delicate hue. Her troubled glance told him she was mentally regrouping—trying to make sense of his request.

'There must be countless important artefacts in a palace this size. Such a project could take months and months. What about my job at the auction house back home?'

'I have no doubt your employers would see it as an honour for one of their staff to undertake this task. There is no doubt in my mind that they will jump at my offer. If you are in agreement with the plan, I will make sure the remuneration you receive is generous.'

'It's not a question of money. What about Jake—I mean Dr Rivers? Do you want to employ him, too?'

A flash of annoyance assailed Zahir that she should mention her colleague. Mockingly he raised his eyebrow. 'No. It is *you* who is the antiquities expert, is it not?'

'I also told you that my father isn't well. I can't just disappear for months on end with no contact.'

Biting back a jealous retort at yet another show of consideration for her father rather than him, Zahir breathed in deeply. Such a response was beneath him.

'You can telephone him and talk to him all you want. I perfectly understand that you need to do that. If he needs a nurse, go ahead and hire one. The palace will foot the bill. As far as Farida is concerned, would you be willing to utilise her help?'

Looking torn, Gina lightly shrugged her shoulders. 'If I undertake to do the inventory, I'm sure her help would be invaluable. Her knowledge of your family treasures must be considerable, having lived with them all her life.'

'Good. Then you agree to do this?'

Zahir could hardly contain his impatience as he waited for her answer. His sister's enthusiasm for Gina's presence had unwittingly given him a legitimate reason to keep her there longer. Now that reason had entered his head he refused to entertain the possibility that his request might be denied.

The big blue eyes still mirrored doubt, but at last she nodded slowly. 'For someone in my profession it's obviously a great opportunity to deepen my knowledge, as well as a privilege—so, yes…I will do it.'

'*Inshallah*… I will make the necessary phone call to the auction house, letting them know what we have agreed.'

'What about the Heart of Courage?'

'Be assured, everything will take its course as it should in that regard. When I have had some time to recuperate we will discuss the rest of your findings concerning the jewel. Now I will send my sister to you here in the library. After that I must go and rest. My doctor will not be happy when he discovers I am not in my bed, where he left me!'

He spun on his heel, grimacing as the sudden movement made him feel as though a sharp-bladed knife had sliced through his ribcage…

It gave Gina a real lift to see less hopelessness and grief in Farida Khan's engaging brown eyes. To be Gina's assistant would give her a purpose, she'd confessed, and knowing that she was helping her beloved brother Zahir, too, would be doubly satisfying.

After the two women had met again in the library, and discussed a plan on how to proceed, Farida had disappeared for a while to locate the necessary keys—keys that would open some of the cabinets that were kept locked. They moved from room to room and floor to floor. She was showing Gina some of the palace's most prized treasures—possessions that were usually only seen by family and close friends. This was to be only a preliminary tour—the work of cataloguing everything would come later—but as she accompanied Farida on her mission to reveal the palace's most revered objects Gina was all but stunned into silence by what she saw.

She knew already how opulently decorated and sumptuous the interior of the palace was—nevertheless room after room seemed to outdo the one before with the riches it revealed, and everywhere she gazed the architecture was a dream. And that was *without* the abundance of extraordinary artefacts hidden away that she was privileged to be shown. Aladdin's Cave had *nothing* on the palace of the Sheikh of Kabuyadir.

Zahir was never far from Gina's mind as she trailed after Farida. *Whenever she thought about his gunshot wounds, she winced and bit her lip.* It was torture to imagine him in pain. Earlier, she had wanted to weep when he didn't kiss her as she'd believed he would. But she'd also been moved that the vivid evidence of his passion the night before had caused him to believe he'd both hurt and offended her. That he cared about that gave her hope. *She didn't want him to forget that they'd shared the most extraordinary connection three years ago that went far beyond mere desire...*

After learning that Jake had gone on a tour of the old part of the town for the evening, Gina ate dinner with Farida. Both women confessed to feeling tired afterwards, so retired to their quarters early.

After reading over her notes, then taking her evening bath, Gina tucked her legs beneath her on the opulent bed and let down her hair. Then she rang her father in the UK. They were three hours ahead here time-wise, so he would still be up and about—in his study working, most likely.

'Professor Collins.'

'Dad, it's me—Gina.'

'What a lovely surprise! How are you getting along in

Kabuyadir? Does it still have the same magic for you that it held last time?'

A little taken aback, she smiled. 'I'm afraid it does—so much so that I've agreed to stay on quite a bit longer than I'd planned. The Sheikh has offered me a job cataloguing some of the more important palace artefacts, as well as presenting my findings on the Heart of Courage.'

'You must have impressed him. That's quite a coup for the auction house as well as you personally.'

'He thinks so, too.' Her comment was wry.

'What's he like…His Highness?'

Gina struggled to find adequate words—especially when all she could really think of was that Zahir was hurting. Was he resting as he should? Might his wounds get infected? Her insides clenched anxiously. But she also had a confession to make.

'I met him once before, Dad,' she admitted softly. 'When I was here the last time. He's the man I told you about—though I didn't know at the time that he was going to inherit his father's title of Sheikh. He's the man I wanted to come back to before Mum died.'

At the other end of the telephone, apart from a few long distance connection crackles, all was silent. 'Dad?'

'Well, well…' he said, and Gina could imagine him rubbing his hand round his jaw and shaking his head in bemusement. 'Do you still care about him, Gina?'

'Yes.' Staring down at the receiver in her hand, she sighed with relief that she'd been able to admit the truth. 'Yes…very much. But he's still angry with me for not coming back when I said I would, and now I don't think he'll ever trust me again.'

'But he's asked you to stay on to catalogue the artefacts? That doesn't sound like a man who has no trust in you, my dear.'

'I'll just have to wait and see how things pan out, won't I?'

She could almost hear her father thinking hard. 'It was selfish of me to stop you going back, Gina. I was distraught about your mother, and fearful of the future without her. Yes, I wanted you to pursue a rewarding career—but I took advantage of your innate kindness to get you to stay at home. I was afraid of losing you to a man thousands of miles away from me. I've since realised what a dreadful thing I did. Now I need to ask *your* forgiveness.'

Tracing one of the swirling patterns on the bed's silk counterpane, Gina swallowed hard. 'There's nothing to forgive, Dad. You needed me, and I chose to stay. Perhaps it just wasn't meant to be...me and Zahir. Anyway, how are *you* doing? Do you mind if I'm away for so long?'

'Mind?' Her father sounded surprised that she would even think it. 'Of course I don't mind! This is a great opportunity for you to make a bit of a name for yourself as well as to advance your career—*if* that's what you want. And if you decide it's Zahir that you want then that's fine, too, and you have my blessing.'

His words stunned her. *He was definitely changing,* she realised. 'Thank you. By the way, how's your new house-keeper working out?'

'To tell you the truth, Lizzie has been an absolute godsend. Not only is she a marvellous cook, but history is one of her passions, too. She's a bright girl...extremely intelligent—and a very good mother to that son of hers. He, by the way, is very bright as well. He's already sorted out that hiccup I had with the computer. Yes, we all get along like a house on fire, so there's no need to worry, Gina. Just give me a ring from time to time and let me know how things are going with you, will you? And don't hesitate to call if you need anything...anything at all.'

Struggling to swallow across the lump in her throat, Gina nodded. After spending many years believing that he scarcely regarded her at all, it was almost overwhelming to hear such love, concern and acceptance in her father's voice. Especially when she considered that she was so far away, and it might be quite a while before they saw each other again.

'I will, Dad.'

'Well, goodbye for now, dear. We'll speak again soon.'

'Bye.'

Drawn to his balcony by the great glowing ball of orange fire that was the sun going down, Zahir experienced the familiar quickening in his blood that was always a given when he witnessed the phenomenon. It made him feel that he was part of much, much more than the mere sights and sounds that daily met his eyes. The realisation humbled him, and he silently gave thanks.

Then the incandescent moment passed and the ache in his side brought him back to more earthly matters—back to the frustration he felt at the thought of being confined by his discomfort for even the shortest time.

Right now he longed for the freedom and vast open spaces of the desert…longed to be pounding along the sand on his beautiful Arabian stallion with the warm wind in his hair and the sun on his back…to forget he was ruler of Kabuyadir for a while. Into his daydream came another tempting facet. On the stallion's back in front of him—his arms keeping her safe—was a woman: the woman who for the past three years had nightly haunted his dreams, the woman who by an incredible quirk of fate was now staying in his palace.

He hadn't written off the idea of making Gina his mistress, despite the fact that he'd said he wouldn't allow his desire to transgress her sense of safety or honour. Tomorrow he would continue his campaign to persuade her—to help her see that it was a natural solution to the inflammatory attraction that gathered force whenever they were together. *If she were to become his mistress he wouldn't have to risk his heart as he had done before,* he told himself. In a way he could hold her at arm's length except for when they were in bed together. Fear of her letting him down again would always ensure he would not wholly trust her.

Even so, his tension lessened a little at the idea she wasn't far away, and that soon—*very* soon—they would share a night together. Zahir released a long slow breath.

'Jamal!'

'Yes, Your Highness.' The loyal servant appeared almost instantly from one of the connecting rooms where he waited on Zahir's instructions—even all through the night.

'I'm going downstairs to the *hamam*. After my bath I will have my usual massage, then I'll need the physician to attend me to rebandage my wounds. Arrange it for me, will you?'

'Straight away, Your Highness.'

Rising shortly after dawn broke, when a full sun had burned away the night and heralded a new day, Gina washed and dressed, then made her way straight to the library. She'd promised to meet Farida after breakfast to make a start on the inventory of palace artefacts, but for now her time was her own.

Browsing the stacked shelves with an intuitive as well as professional nose, she retrieved four heavy volumes of history of the area and carried them to the long varnished table beneath a row of narrow windows. The air echoed with the spine-tingling sound of the Muezzin, calling the faithful to prayer, and Gina shut her eyes for a moment to absorb the ancient chant more fully. Then she opened the first great book in the pile she'd laid on the table.

Moroccan-style brass lamps on the walls were still glowing softly from the night before, and even though the sun was already blazing, the extra light definitely helped illuminate the hushed cathedral dimness of the area. There were several interesting references to Zahir's dynastic family, and what she read kept Gina enthralled for at least a couple of hours. Finally realising the time, she quickly returned the books to the correct shelves and all but fled back down the maze of lofty gilded corridors to the terrace, where she'd breakfast with Jake.

'Morning, Gina... I heard you were hobnobbing with the Sheikh's widowed sister yesterday. What's she like? Is she as striking in appearance as her imposing brother, or did she get the short straw in the looks department?'

'For goodness' sake, Jake, where are your manners? What if Jamal heard you?' Gina looked daggers at her tactless colleague, then anxiously swept her gaze round the terrace to see if Zahir's faithful man was nearby. Thankfully, he wasn't. Only the two girls who served the food stood silently by the sandstone wall, waiting to be of assistance.

Already helping himself to the colourful generous repast that was arranged on the table, Jake returned an unrepentant glance. 'It's only natural that I should be curious. I gather the general consensus in these parts is that she'll never marry again. Something to do with that prophecy that so fascinates you—she was head over heels in love with her husband and won't give her heart to anyone else. Not in this lifetime anyway.'

At this reminder of the prophecy, Gina's own heart seemed to turn over in her chest. It wasn't hard for her to understand Farida's vow, should it be true. If she couldn't be with Zahir then she, too, would probably live out the rest of her days alone.

'Seems a terrible waste, though, doesn't it?'

'What does?'

'I think this place is hypnotising you! You've increasingly got that faraway look in your eyes. It's going to be hard when you return to good old Blighty, isn't it? Back home to the *real* world.'

Falling silent, Gina helped herself to some bread and a few olives. Soon she would have to tell Jake about the extra job Zahir had asked her to do—but not yet. She wanted the chance to complete her presentation on the Heart of Courage first. When Jake's work was also completed, and he was thinking about travelling home, then she would tell him. The man was so ambitious that for all she knew he might be funny with her because she'd been asked to undertake the inventory and he hadn't. It definitely wasn't above him to be jealous and petty about her perceived good fortune.

'It is another world here, isn't it?' She forced herself to be sociable and friendly.

'By the way, there's the most bizarre rumour going round that the Sheikh was shot by some rebels the other day when he went to try and make peace with them. He wasn't killed, obviously, just wounded. This place is like some kind of paradise lost, but I still get the feeling that anything could go off at any time, don't you? I didn't see him at all yesterday. Do you think the rumours are true?'

Schooling her expression to stay calm, Gina swallowed some food, then delicately touched her napkin to her lips. 'I don't think we should speculate about it. If it is true then I only hope the poor man is resting and recuperating as he needs to, so that he can heal.'

'I don't like to think we won't be able to finish our

presentations if he really is laid up with a gunshot wound. We've both worked hard these past two months. I don't want it all to be for nothing.'

Finally Gina lost patience. Pushing to her feet, she glared at the man, who was dressed in another inappropriately garish shirt this morning. 'Don't you *ever* think about anybody but yourself? The palace has paid for you to travel first class, and we've been waited on hand and foot, as well as receiving a generous advance for our research on the Heart of Courage. I'd hardly call that "nothing", would you?'

Throwing her napkin on top of her plate, she marched away, leaving the two sweet girls who had been assigned to serve them staring at her as if she was a species from another planet.

In his study on one of the upper floors, the sound of girlish laughter reached his ears. Frowning in puzzlement, Zahir moved across to the sandstone and mosaic embrasure and glanced out. There were two women seated at the marble inlaid table in the intimate courtyard below, where a silk canopy protected them from the fierce midday sun. One wore the traditional black garb of a widow, and the other a long coral silk dress with a loose white overshirt and an incongruous straw hat that made him smile.

Seeing them together, clearly enjoying each other's company, was a revelation. *Rarely had a sight and sound given him more pleasure.* Without knowing he'd intended it, he found himself outside, approaching the table where they sat. When the women started to rise from their seats he gestured for them to stay where they were.

'I was beginning to fear I would never see you smile or hear you laugh again, my sister.'

'It is all Gina's doing. See how good she is for me? Not

only is she clever and kind, but she has a wicked sense of humour, too.'

'Is that so?' Immediately Zahir's interested glance moved from his sister to the fair-skinned woman seated by her side. Her lovely blue eyes had been brimming with humour just a few moments ago, but now, beneath his scrutiny, her expression turned serious. He didn't know why, but it grieved him.

'Good afternoon, Your Highness,' she murmured.

'You are looking very well, Dr Collins.' He smiled. 'Like a rose plucked from an English country garden and planted out here in the desert.'

'Such a rose probably wouldn't survive in this heat.'

'If it was tended and looked after by an expert gardener, I have no doubt it would blossom.'

Helplessly, he fell into a trance, his skin prickling hotly with languorous need. He ignored the fact that his sister was staring at him speculatively. Then Gina reached out to gather up some papers that were strewn across the table, and Zahir snapped out of the hypnotised spell that had overcome him.

'I will let you get back to your conversation. I apologise for disturbing you both,' he muttered, then turned abruptly and strode away.

As his dark robes flew out behind him, his booted footsteps ringing out across the paved courtyard, Farida frowned. 'My brother does not seem at all like his usual self this morning. It could be that he has suffered a sleepless night because of his wounds. You know he was wounded in a skirmish with some rebels the other day?'

'Yes…I heard what happened. It was a shock.' Lowering her lashes, Gina tried to scan some of the notes she had made with regard to the inventory that was underway, but all she saw on the screen of her mind was the disturbing heat in Zahir's riveting dark eyes. It made her press her thighs together beneath her dress, because suddenly she ached to the very core of her being for his ardent lovemaking.

Inevitably, she remembered the night she had surrendered her virginity. The erotic electricity their bodies had generated had been so powerful, so magnetising, that when he had penetrated her she hadn't experienced the slightest pain or discomfort. Their bonding had been so perfect, so natural, that she had no doubt it had been written in the stars...

Realising that Farida was waiting for her opinion, Gina strove for a reassuring smile. 'Your brother...His Highness...is clearly a very strong, fit man, and I've no doubt that he'll make a full and speedy recovery.'

The other woman shrugged. 'That is what I tell myself, too. But no matter how strong he is, he is not infallible. No one is. This house has known too much death of late. It needs new blood to revitalise it and give us hope. Perhaps it is a good thing that Zahir intends to marry soon. Even if I cannot agree with his bride of choice.'

Feeling as if her breath had been seared inside her lungs, Gina stared in shock. 'The Sheikh is getting married?'

Farida sighed and nodded. 'His intended is an Emir's daughter. She is plump and plain, and I'm sorry to say not very clever. Thank Allah he is not looking for scintillating company, because he won't enjoy such a thing with her. No... He has only seen the girl once or twice, but her family rule a great kingdom, too. It is a marriage of convenience my brother has planned, and I see nothing but pain and unhappiness ahead for him should he go through with it.'

It was hard for Gina to speak because of the dryness in her throat. 'But what about the Heart of Courage's prophecy that all your family will marry for love, not dynastic advantage?'

'You know about the jewel?'

She'd forgotten she wasn't supposed to mention it to Farida. Her heart raced as she quickly sought to explain. 'Knowing I was going to undertake an inventory of the palace artefacts, I did some research before I came and discovered the existence of the jewel. It's got quite a history.'

Leaning forward, Farida grabbed Gina's hand. 'I totally believe in the prophecy! One cannot and should not argue with fate. As soon as I set eyes on Azhar I knew it was meant that we should meet and fall in love. In fact I loved him from the very first moment, and I will not stop loving him for the rest of my life—even though he is gone from me. My heart keeps him alive. Do you understand?'

'I do... I believe everything you say, Farida. But your brother...? He doesn't believe in the prophecy?'

'He does not. I have tried to talk to Zahir many times about it, but he will not listen. Because my parents married for love, and my father pined for my mother so much when she died that he himself passed away shortly after, and then I sadly lost Azhar, he is scared to experience a love so profound in case he will be a broken man if he should lose it. There is no convincing him otherwise. He can be very stubborn at times—especially when he thinks he is right!'

'So he would rather marry someone he barely knows or cares about instead?'

The other girl sadly dipped her head. 'It would seem so.'

Walking in a semi-daze down the corridor later, her notes clutched to her chest, Gina didn't even register a door opening until a deep male voice uttered her name.

'Gina.' Holding the study door wide, Zahir commanded her with his piercing dark gaze.

'Don't you mean Dr Collins, Your Highness?' It was almost impossible to keep the hurt from her voice when all she could think was that he was marrying a woman he hardly knew, purely for dynastic alliance. Of all the things she had ever suffered, surely this was the hardest to bear of all?

CHAPTER SEVEN

'I WISH to speak with you.'

'I'm sorry, but I can't spare the time right now. I have too much work to do.'

Gina barely knew where she found the temerity to speak to him like that, but she supposed hurt and anger instigated it. The fiercely warning glance Zahir gave her in return was enough to quell the courage of Ghengis Khan himself, and she couldn't deny that her legs weren't shaking.

'How dare you address me in such a manner? Such disrespect would be enough to have you incarcerated. In future I would advise you to think twice before succumbing to it. Come into my study...*now*.'

Closing the door behind them, Zahir gestured to Gina to take a seat. *She was glad of it*. Laying down her papers on a lavish brocade-covered couch, she folded her hands in her lap, took a deep breath, then made herself meet his glowering gaze.

'I apologise sincerely if I was rude, Your Highness. It won't happen again. What is it you want to talk to me about?'

Hands behind his back, he paced the marble floor, his handsome profile ominously formidable as his boot heels rang out against the stone. When he came to a stop, but still didn't speak, a jolt of fear zigzagged through her.

'What's wrong? Are you in pain?' she asked.

A curse violently left his lips. Striding up to her, he hauled her to her feet. Suddenly finding herself on the most personal and intimate terms with his flashing eyes, warm breath and steely strength as he gripped her arms, Gina was shocked by how faint with longing for him she was.

'Yes, I *am* in pain! I am in pain not because of a gunshot wound but because I have had to endure not having the taste of your mouth whenever I desire it, not having your body naked beneath mine! Can you even imagine what I am going through because you deny me these things? Or are you so heartless that you don't even care?'

'Zahir, I do care. I—'

Any words she had been about to say were cut off by the hot pressure of his mouth on hers. Groaning, Gina wound her arms round his neck, and he was like a rock or the trunk of a tree she could hang on to for dear life were she in danger of being swept away by a hurricane.

In turn, Zahir held her fast as his tongue tangled hotly with hers, moving his hands up and down her back as he tried to position her closer, even closer, until there was no space between them and they were but one passionate beating heart. Reaching up, he freed her hair, and it spilled curling and golden round her shoulders.

He had said that *he* had had to endure surviving without the taste of her lips, the intimacy of her body against his... Gina didn't even know how to *start* telling him she felt the same. All she could do was demonstrate her wildly hungry feelings by matching him kiss for ravenous kiss, her hands as greedy for the touch of his skin as his for hers. His body was hard as iron beneath his flowing robes, his mouth a passionate burning brand that left her heart no choice but to be enslaved by him for ever.

Breathing hard, he broke off the kiss to cup her face

between his hands. 'I must have you in my bed tonight...
After this, can you still deny me?'

Thinking was hardly possible right then, while Gina's
body still throbbed from the delicious intimacy of Zahir's
passionate embrace, and her senses were frustrated at not
having her craving for him completely fulfilled. But, like a
serpent in paradise, an unhappily wounding thought reared
its dangerous head and wouldn't be ignored.

'Release me.'

'What?' Confusion and not a little frustration filled his
eyes.

'You have to let me go. I—I need to sit down for a
minute.'

As soon as Zahir set her free Gina sank down onto
the brocade couch, her mouth drying uncomfortably at the
question that had reared commandingly inside her head—a
question she desperately needed an answer to.

'Your sister told me today that you are soon to be married. She said it is to be an arranged marriage to an Emir's
daughter. Is that true, Zahir?'

His glittering gaze considered her bleakly for a moment,
then he spun away to pace the floor again. A couple of feet
away from her he stilled. A shaft of sunlight beaming in
through a narrow window alighted on the mane of long hair
that spilled across his shoulders, and the copper lights deep
within the fiercely glossy ebony strands glinted like dark
fire. In her wildest dreams Gina couldn't have dreamed up
a man more magnificent—or more *unattainable*.

'It is true... But what has that to do with us? I am not
marrying her for her beautiful body, or her wit and charm,
so there is nothing to be jealous about if jealousy is what
you feel—not when you possess all those attributes in
abundance. It is, as you say, merely an arranged union for

dynastic purposes only. The arranged marriage is common enough amongst titled landowners in these parts.'

'The last time you explained about that you hadn't found anyone suitable. Obviously things have moved on quickly since then?'

'Look…whether I marry this woman or not has nothing to do with what *we* share. Absolutely nothing! Why can you not see that?'

Capturing a strand of the bright hair that drifted round her shoulders, Gina coiled it round her finger, then let it spring free. 'Why can't I see that?' A soft, wounded sigh escaped her. 'Perhaps because I firmly believe that marriage should be one man for one woman, and that the relationship should have love as its foundation…not convenience or—or sex!' Gathering up her scattered papers from the cushion beside her, she pushed to her feet. 'If you'll excuse me, I must get on. I've promised to meet up with your sister again, and I need to pop up to my room for a book first.'

Zahir was back in front of her in an instant. A myriad of passionate emotions swirled and flickered in the silken depths of his long-lashed eyes. 'Know this…I do not ask you to become my mistress because I do not care for you. Even though you hurt me with your false promise to return, there is no other woman I desire or want to be close to but you, Gina.'

Biting down on her lip, she resisted the strongest urge to touch her hand lovingly to his high-contoured cheekbone. She hadn't forgotten that he'd recently been shot at and might have lost his life. 'I believe you, Zahir.'

'Then why shut me out as you clearly *are* doing?'

'Because even though you say you care for me, it's not enough to persuade me to either share your bed again or become your mistress. I don't want to play second fiddle to another woman, even though you might not hold her in high regard and your marriage would be just a formality…a convenience. I would be betraying my own integrity *and* hers if I do that, and that's important to me. I'm sorry, Zahir, but that's just how I feel.'

Leaving him standing there, his expression stunned and sombre, she moved across to the door and went out.

After Gina had so shockingly deserted him, Zahir bellowed for Jamal and gave him orders to get his Arabian stallion saddled up, ready for his immediate use. Less than half an hour later, ignoring his concerned manservant's plea to not ride too far lest he tear open his wounds, he mounted the magnificent ebony steed and rode off into the hills.

What else could he do with all the restless and unsatisfied desire that thrummed through his veins? He had to burn some of that raging fire in him away or else he would certainly go mad. And he couldn't abide staying at the palace and twiddling his thumbs for the afternoon just because his doctor had advised him to rest…not after Gina's unbelievable rebuff.

Why was the woman being so stubborn? It seriously perplexed him. There was an old saying: *patience is beautiful*… Right now he was far too frustrated and furious to contemplate the wisdom it was no doubt meant to impart. What would entice her to become his mistress, to realise it would give her far greater access to his body and his time than any plain, unimaginative eighteen-year-old wife, who would rather giggle with her girlfriends and feed her face than learn how to pleasure a man?

When Zahir glanced round to see a palace bodyguard following him on another steed, he let loose an oath. Giving the horse his head, he stirred him into a brisk canter. Then, when they were out in more open country, into a full heart-pounding gallop…

* * *

'Turn around.' Farida's look of quiet concentration was endearing as she watched Gina model the black *hijab* and dress that she'd loaned her, so that she could accompany herself and a male servant to the market.

After that emotional scene with Zahir in his study earlier, the unexpected trip Farida had suggested was the perfect antidote to the melancholic feelings that kept washing over her. It hurt deeply that she was apparently good enough to be Zahir's mistress but *not* his wife. Yet, underlying the sensation of despondency, she held on to the fact that he had at least declared he cared for her. Maybe that knowledge would give Gina something to work with? Thinking of the personal search she had started in the library, she yearned to get back there soon.

'From behind you will look just like any other young woman visiting the marketplace. It is only when people see your fair skin and sapphire-blue eyes they will know you are not a native from Kabuyadir.'

'I rather like the anonymity these clothes give you,' Gina remarked thoughtfully, running her hand down over the smooth black silk. 'Back at home women are bombarded daily by the media with what we should look like, what size we should be and what clothes we should wear—usually revealing ones. It's a refreshing change not to worry about that for once.'

'Well, I am glad they make you feel more at ease. We will have a good visit... You will enjoy it and so will I. This will be my first outing for a long time. Now, if there is anything you want at the marketplace—for instance souvenirs or a length of silk or brocade to make a dress— let my servant barter for you. That is how it is done here, and it will ensure you get a good price.'

The marketplace was a sensation overload. Turning her head this way and that, Gina endeavoured to absorb as much of the sights and sounds as possible. When she was back in the UK, doing her weekly shop at the supermarket or visiting some soulless shopping mall for some so-called 'retail therapy,' buying clothes she didn't really want that would disappear amongst similar impulse buys in her wardrobe, she would certainly long for Kabuyadir and all the fascinating goods that made the market so much more exotic and appealing—so much more *authentic*, somehow.

Staying close by her side, Farida was the best guide she could have had. As well as pointing out various stalls that might be of interest—whether their vendors were selling colourful silks, yarns and brocades, handmade rugs or the beautifully crafted ceramics that so many visitors made a beeline for—she often added humorous little anecdotes that made Gina smile.

After about an hour of negotiating their way through the melee of people, with their colourful clothes and many languages littering the sultry air, Farida thankfully suggested they take a break for some refreshments. Coming upon a group of chairs and tables beneath a tall date palm tree, she despatched her servant Hafiz to the stallholder who was serving drinks and sweetmeats.

'Is there anything you have seen that you like enough to take home?' her companion asked as they sat together with their backs to the refreshment stall.

'I noticed a vendor selling essential oils... I'd definitely be interested in taking some agarwood oil home—the scent is divine. It will always remind me of Kabuyadir.' *And Zahir*, she thought with a bittersweet tug.

'We will visit his stall after our refreshments—but I will only allow you to purchase the oil if I know it is of the highest grade.'

'Thanks. You've been very good to me, Farida... I just want you to know how much I appreciate it.'

''Nonsense! You have been like a breath of fresh air to me, Gina, and I thank you for agreeing to spend time with a dull and sombre woman like me.'

'You are not dull *or* sombre…you mustn't put yourself down like that. I wish I had as good and bright and engaging a friend as you at home. When I eventually return there you'll always be welcome to visit and stay with me at any time.'

'That pleases me very much—but do not talk about leaving Kabuyadir yet, I beg you!'

'I'm not in a hurry to leave at all, as I'm sure you—' Gina didn't finish the sentence. An arm that felt like iron had grabbed her round the neck from behind, and the smell of stale masculine sweat enveloped her.

A strangled yelp left her throat as she was dragged violently from her chair, even as Farida screamed for Hafiz. Her hands fastened on the coffee-coloured forearm of the man she now realised with sickening shock was trying to abduct her, and pure adrenaline-fuelled reaction—and not a little indignant fury—made her sink her teeth into the smooth hard flesh and bite him hard. Immediately he let her go, cursing loudly. By then Hafiz was on the scene, along with a crowd of shrieking, excitable onlookers, and the well-built servant and another man grappled the assailant to the ground and held him fast.

'Gina! Are you all right?'

Farida was as stunned and shaken as she was. Even though her answer was an affirmative nod, Gina sensed the violent aftershocks of her assault roll through her, and she couldn't stop shaking. It was hard to believe that such an out-of-the-blue frightening occurrence had happened here in broad daylight, in a busy marketplace.

'I'm okay…I think. But I—I do need to sit down.'

A chair was quickly positioned behind her, and someone

pushed through the crowd to put a bottle of water into her hand with the halting instruction. 'Please do drink.'

Instantly Farida took the bottle, opened it, and sniffed the contents. 'It's okay. You can drink it—it will help.' She returned it to Gina.

With Farida's encouragement she downed the water in one, and the dryness in her mouth, as well as her shock, eased a little.

Someone had yelled for the security forces, and as if by magic officers peeled out of nowhere into the crowded market, swarming round the man who had dragged Gina from her chair. The assailant was young, but she blanched when she saw the seriously lethal-looking sharp-bladed knife that was retrieved from beneath his long robes.

'Who is he?' Her voice was decidedly shaky as she met Farida's concerned brown eyes. 'Why would he do this?'

'I don't know, my friend. But you can be sure of one thing…my brother will find out who he is and who put him up to this before you can blink an eyelid!'

Hafiz returned. Bowing courteously to both women, he turned his worried gaze specifically on Gina. Clearly frustrated at not being able to converse with her in English, he turned back to Farida, addressing the Sheikh's sister rapidly and urgently in their own language.

She sighed and said, 'Hafiz is distraught that he did not protect you better, Gina. I have told him it was not his fault. None of us was remotely aware of any danger as we made our way through the market.'

'You're not to blame, Hafiz. There's no need for an apology, really.'

'It is *I* who is to blame,' Farida insisted. 'My brother will go crazy when he learns that I took you to the market without taking a bodyguard with us. I can't have been thinking clearly. In the light of what happened to Zahir I should have realised that it might not be completely safe. But, Gina, you were so brave—biting the attacker like that. If you had not, I shudder to think what might have happened.'

'You're not to blame, either, Farida. And I prefer to deal with what *is* than speculate on what might have been. I'm okay, aren't I? I'm still here—alive and kicking.' Injecting some firmness into her tone, Gina even made herself smile—the last thing she wanted was the other woman berating herself for the incident, even if the truth was that her nerves were as scrambled as if she'd leapt from a fast-moving train.

'You remind me of Zahir when you say that. He had a similar reaction when I told him that he could have been killed by that gunman. "But I *wasn't*," he said…' Eyeing Gina with a definitely speculative glance, Farida stood in front of her and held out a hand to help her to her feet. 'I will talk to the public security forces and then we will go directly home.'

The hard ride on his stallion had partially torn open the wound on Zahir's side. Biting back a soft curse as his disapproving physician put in fresh stitches, he was nonetheless unrepentant. The ride had not only helped divert some of his frustration and restless energy, but had also helped clear his head.

As much as his proud, fiercely masculine nature and privileged position made him want to demand that Gina share his bed, he sensed that that was definitely *not* the way to go about achieving his goal. After all, he didn't want to alienate her or make her hate him. No…instead he would employ a charm offensive that she couldn't resist.

To start with he would give her a private showing of the Heart of Courage—even before he let her colleague Dr Rivers see the artefact. Then he would organise a special dinner for two in the palace's grandest dining room, where she would marvel at the opulence and grandeur of the furnishings and—

'A thousand pardons, Your Highness.' The double doors flew wide and Jamal strode purposefully into the room. His urgent tone and agitated expression immediately applied the emergency brake to Zahir's distracted train of thought. He'd been lying back against the luxurious satin pillows on his bed whilst his doctor snipped the thread from the last stitch he'd applied, but now he sat up abruptly. 'What is it? What's happened?'

In a heated rush, Jamal told him. It was as though he'd been punched in the stomach by an iron fist. *Gina...* For a disturbing few seconds his thoughts were so distressed by the idea she might be hurt that Zahir was paralysed. Then, as Jamal continued to regale him with the story of how Dr Collins had almost been abducted in the marketplace, where she'd gone with Farida and his sister's servant Hafiz, he swung his muscular legs to the floor and grabbed the long black robes he'd been wearing from the end of the bed—deliberately ignoring his physician's plea to wait until his wounds were rebandaged as he hastily dressed.

Inside his chest his heart mimicked the heavy thud of a steel hammer against stone. *Had he visited this latest calamity on his family by thinking he could apply reason to his dealings with the rebels?* It had already been demonstrated what a deluded belief that was! Would his father have simply sent in the military to sort them out, giving them no chance to state their grievances whatsoever? Had Zahir's arrogance in believing his way was right diminished his wisdom?

Shutting out the bittersweet memory of his father—a man who had been affectionately admired by officials and the public alike for his wisdom and fairness when dealing with matters of governance—he hurried out through the door at a mile a minute, with no mind to Jamal who, although young and fit, panted a little in his bid to keep pace with him.

The women were in a private downstairs salon, where they were drinking tea. On entering the lavishly decorated room, with its long gold-coloured couches and antique furniture, Zahir let his anxious glance deliberately overshoot his sister to dwell first on the slender, fair-haired woman seated at her side. Her usual tidy French pleat was a little awry, and escaping curling tendrils framed the delicate beauty of her face to give her the same vulnerable look that Zahir remembered from their first meeting in the Husseins' garden. His breath caught in his throat.

In contrast the plain, traditional long black dress she wore hardly seemed fitting for such incandescent loveliness. He guessed it belonged to his sister. His first desire was to go straight to Gina, but because Farida and her servant Hafiz were both present he didn't.

'What is this I have been hearing about an assault on Dr Collins in the marketplace?' he demanded, not bothering to temper his outrage.

Both Hafiz and his sister flinched. 'It happened so quickly, Zahir. There was nothing we could—'

'Nothing you could do?' he interrupted furiously, uncaring in that moment that Farida looked distraught. 'Why didn't you take a bodyguard with you? In fact, why did you not take two—one for each of you? Have you forgotten what happened to me just the other day? For the love of Allah, what possessed you to go to the market in the first place? If you had wanted something specifically you could have sent your servant!'

'I'm sorry, Your Highness, but I can't sit here and let

your sister take the blame for something that happened totally out of the blue.'

Having risen to her feet—a little shakily, he noticed with alarm—Gina all but pierced Zahir's soul with the fiercely protective glint of her blue eyes. She continually astonished him. No more than now, as she refused to let him berate Farida for undertaking a trip she hadn't needed to make in the first place, thereby putting them both at grave risk.

'As lovely as it is, we both needed to get out of the palace for a while. When Farida suggested a trip to the marketplace I jumped at the chance. So if you're intent on blaming your sister, then I want you to know that I am equally to blame.'

'Did the assailant hurt you?' He couldn't help the catch in his voice. Right then he didn't care who noted it, either. It was hell to stand there and pretend his concern was only that of a respectful host for a guest who had suffered some accident or mishap whilst under his roof when all the while he wanted to hold Gina in his arms and ascertain for himself whether she was hurt or not.

'The man grabbed Gina from behind and dragged her from her chair. I am certain his aim was to abduct her, but fortunately she reacted quickly and bit him. He cursed and let her go,' Farida explained, colouring slightly.

'You *bit* him?' Was it possible for this woman to amaze him any further? Arms akimbo, Zahir stared.

'It was purely instinctive. I'm no heroine, I assure you.'

'The law enforcement officers found a dangerous-looking knife under the man's robes.'

His sister glanced at Gina with what looked to be an apologetic shrug, but it was too late. Zahir's mind had already delved into the most horrific scenarios at news of the attack *without* the information that the assailant had been carrying a knife.

'And the officers interviewed you for details of the assault on Dr Collins?' His voice sounded strangely disembodied to his own ears, as shock and mounting fury spilled through his veins.

'They did. They'll be here shortly to have a meeting with you, Zahir. Do you think it was anything to do with the rebels?'

'I do not doubt it.' Scowling, Zahir dropped his hands to his hips. Helplessly, he returned his concerned hungry glance to Gina. Her skin had turned the sickly pallor of oatmeal, and suddenly, frighteningly, it was clear to him that she was having trouble keeping her balance.

'Gina!' Rushing forward, he caught her slim body in his arms just before she hit the marble floor.

CHAPTER EIGHT

As HE kicked open the door of Gina's bedroom, to carry her across to the emperor-sized bed with its purple silk counterpane, Zahir realised he had an entourage. His sister, two servants—not including Jamal—and finally Dr Saffar, the personal physician he had commanded Jamal to fetch straight away, followed him.

Laying his precious cargo carefully down on the bed, he personally removed her shoes, then sat on the edge of the counterpane beside her, the tension inside him building excruciatingly every moment her eyes stayed closed. Taking her hand in his, he could not hide his shock at how cold it was. Moving to the other side of the bed, his physician lightly slapped Gina's pale cheeks.

Realising they were being watched, Zahir irritably waved his audience away. 'Go. Leave us!'

'May I stay?' His sister had tears in her eyes.

'Of course.' He didn't apologise for his clipped-sounding tone. His whole being was focused on one thing and one thing only...*Gina*.

As he turned back the doctor was cradling her head and moving a bottle of smelling salts back and forth beneath her nose. Her eyelids quivered then opened thankfully wide to reveal dazzling blue irises.

'What happened?'

'You fainted, my dear.'

The physician's avuncular tone surprised Zahir. The only person he had addressed quite as kindly before was his sister Farida.

'It can happen sometimes after a bad shock.'

'I've never fainted before.'

'There is a first time for everything, and it is nothing to worry about.'

The man smiled again, and Zahir was almost jealous that he was the one to comfort and reassure Gina. But then her worried glance collided with his, and this time he made sure it was *his* smile she was the recipient of.

Cupping her cold hand, he lightly stroked it. 'You frightened me,' he said simply.

Pursing her lips, she didn't attempt to speak, but he sensed her hand curl deliberately into his palm and his heart leapt.

'Now, I am afraid that you will have to leave us for a while, Your Highness… I need to properly examine Dr Collins.' The physician was opening his medical bag. Peering over the rims of his spectacles, he looked straight at Farida across Zahir's shoulder. 'You may stay and assist me, Your Highness.'

Outside in the silent corridor, Zahir crossed his arms over his chest and paced, grim-faced. A wind was getting up outside. Through the apertures in the narrow windows, it disturbed the glass and brass lanterns hanging from the ceiling and made them tinkle like windchimes.

After what seemed like an interminable period, Farida opened the door. Her smooth forehead was disturbed by a somewhat sad frown. 'Dr Saffar says you may come back in now.'

'Is she hurt?' he demanded.

His sister's frown deepened. 'She has some bad bruising

either side of her neck and on her collarbone, but the doctor has given me some salve I may apply to help soothe the soreness. I don't think she registered she was hurt at the time…it was more the psychological shock that affected her. But, Zahir…'

'What is it?'

'I think whoever did this may have mistaken Gina for me. We were both sitting with our backs to the refreshment stall—we are of similar size, and she was wearing one of my dresses and a *hijab*. We were with Hafiz, who had the palace insignia on his tunic, and I am known in Kabuyadir and she is not. What reason would the rebels have for taking *her?*'

'None that I can immediately think of.' He fisted his hands and swore. Rubbing at his temples, he stared at the woman in front of him. 'It sounds to me like this was a totally opportunist act—not one that was orchestrated. Else why did the assailant act alone in the middle of a crowded marketplace? No… He must have seen Hafiz with the two of you, noted the palace insignia on his tunic and aimed to ingratiate himself with his leader by trying to kidnap you to get at me. The idea of someone abducting you sends a shudder though my soul, but I am equally furious that they hurt Gina—who is, after all, an innocent bystander.' The wheels of Zahir's mind were rapidly spinning with thoughts of what to do next.

'She will make a good recovery I am sure, brother. She is strong, and today I have seen for myself she's a *fighter.*'

Even though he privately concurred with his sister's summation, it didn't prevent his insides from twisting agonisingly at the thought of that uncouth rebel half strangling her. As sure as Allah's will reigned supreme he and his leader would pay and pay *dearly.* And so would anybody associated with them. This time Zahir would neither be in the mood nor the market for reasoning—in any shape or form...

'Your Highness, the captain of the security forces is downstairs, waiting for an audience with you.' As he walked hurriedly towards them, from the other end of the lofty corridor, Jamal's usually calm demeanour was a little flustered.

'Tell him I will be with him shortly.' Giving his servant the barest glance as he snapped out the instruction, he gestured to his sister to precede him back into Gina's room. 'First I must ascertain for myself how Dr Collins fares.'

Zahir had said little to Gina when he'd returned to see her after her examination. How could he when they'd had an audience of his sister and Dr Saffar? But his eyes—those deep, dark, silken orbs—had spoken *volumes* as they'd studied her. In turn she had felt as if she was developing an incurable fever—a fever that no medicine could cure because the only cure for her malady was *him*.

He'd indicated that he was going crazy, not being able to be alone with her, and she echoed the feeling with every fibre of her being. Even more so now, after she'd been grabbed by that madman in the marketplace! Now she wanted to grab onto Zahir—to have him exhibit his passion in the most uninhibited feral way—so that she could convince herself she'd survived that attack—still lived, still breathed—and that someone *cared,* truly cared, that she had.

In a deeply luxurious armchair in a corner of the room Farida sat silently, absorbed in some intricate-looking embroidery. At any other time the simple, peaceful movements of needle and thread going in and out of the gold and white silk runner she was sewing would have lulled Gina into relaxing.

Sensing her glance from where she lay, resting on the bed, the other girl lifted her pretty mouth in a smile. 'Are you okay? Do you need anything?'

Gina shook her head, with the barest of smiles back. It was such a loaded question. What else could she do when what she needed most of all was Zahir? 'I feel ridiculously pampered and spoiled, lying in bed like this, so—no... there's nothing I need right now, Farida...thank you.'

'You must be the most undemanding patient in the world, Gina. After what you suffered this afternoon you could ask for anything and Zahir and I would try to get it for you.'

'Talking of your brother—His Highness—will he join us for dinner tonight?'

'I'm afraid not, Gina. He has some important business to attend to. He left in a bit of a hurry with the captain of the security forces and told me he didn't know when he would be back. In the meantime he left strict instructions that you were not to lift so much as a finger. Dr Saffar suggested you should have a tray brought up to your room rather than endure a more formal dinner, and I agree with him. We all want to make sure you are fully recovered from your ordeal before even the slightest demands are made of you.'

Swallowing down her crushing disappointment that she wouldn't see Zahir for the entire evening, Gina drew her knees up beneath the counterpane, then wrapped her arms round them. 'And what about Dr Rivers? Did anybody tell him what happened?'

'Yes, he was told. He was very shocked. He told Jamal to tell you that he would see you when you felt more recovered.'

She grimaced at that. It was typical of Jake not to disturb himself with hearing the details of what had happened to her, and also not to want to see her in case she was distressed. He wasn't the kind of man who could cope with any kind of display of female emotion. But in a way Gina was relieved. Spending time with her colleague when she was fit and well was taxing enough, never mind when she wasn't...

In the light of the single brass lamp beside the bed Gina drifted off to sleep after another meal she had barely touched. In the far distance the strains of some haunting melody played on an *oud* reached her ears. Eventually it lulled her to sleep. But the dreams that visited her were not the kind of dreams that ensured her rest was peaceful.

When the memory of a cruel strong arm round her neck replayed itself with frightening clarity, she bolted upright with shock. As her gaze adjusted to the dim lighting she saw that Farida was no longer ensconced in the armchair. Someone else had taken her place. It was *Zahir*...

Her heart thudding, she tried to rub the sleep from her eyes to focus better on the dark, haunting face that was almost in complete shadow.

'I could not stay away, *rohi*. Did you think I could?'

He got up from the chair and came to the bedside. To Gina's captivated senses his shoulders seemed extra wide tonight, and he was tall—so tall. His hypnotic dark eyes and disturbingly handsome features had never been so powerfully affecting and beguiling. With his unbound ebony hair and the black robes that covered his strong masculine form he resembled nothing less than a mythical prince—a prince who had perhaps reigned here at the same time as the necklace that held the Heart of Courage was created.

'I'm glad you came,' she whispered.

The tips of his fingers softly grazed her cheek. 'I want to take you somewhere. Are you up to making a small trip?'

'A trip where?'

'Not far.' Gentle humour briefly stretched the corners of his mouth.

Needing no second bidding, Gina swung her legs over the side of the bed. Some time between her eating her meal and falling asleep Farida had helped her into one of her long white cotton nightgowns. The material clung to her bare body underneath, then fell away down to the floor as Zahir helped her to her feet.

'You will need your slippers,' he instructed, smiling. He held her hand as she reached down for the soft sequinned shoes beside the bed and slipped them on.

They walked beneath the shadowed light of a crescent moon through the gardens. The powerfully drugging scents of jasmine and orange blossom infiltrated Gina's blood as they moved silently beneath grand mosaic arches towards a destination that was unfamiliar to her.

Ahead of her, in an enclosed private garden, an open fire glowed fiercely, hissing sparks like the forge from a smithy. Just behind it an imposing Bedouin tent rose up. Above them the inky night sky was peppered with a million, zillion stars...too many to count.

She glanced sidelong at Zahir. His hand still firmly held onto hers. 'Who sleeps here?'

There was a glimpse of strong white teeth amid the dark shadow of his face. 'I do.'

At his instigation, Gina preceded him inside the tent. She gasped at the wondrous atmosphere that greeted her invitingly—an atmosphere created by the hand-woven walls and ceiling, the medley of satin and silk pillows liberally scattered, and the colourful, intricately patterned hand-stitched rugs that covered the floor. Apart from the glow of the open fire, a single Moroccan lamp with a flickering candle burning inside was the only illumination. The shadows it threw onto the material walls mesmerised and danced like ghosts.

Moving across the soft rug-covered floor, she turned to rest her back against one of the sumptuous pillows. 'It's so beautiful…' Her voice was respectfully hushed, as though she had sneaked inside a church in the middle of the night. 'Magical.'

Saying nothing, Zahir reached for the topmost corner of the tent flap and closed the opening that had been there previously. Then he took off his long leather boots and, briefly opening the tent flap again, put them outside. Crawling over to her on all fours, he carefully, silently removed Gina's slippers and laid them aside. Then, bending his dark head, he reverently kissed her feet.

That simple, astonishing act released the flood of emotion she'd been desperately trying to hold back for days, and when he raised his gaze to hers she could hardly find her voice to speak. Instead, she simply held out her arms for him to fill them. His kiss when it came was satin and fire, summer heat and electrical storm. It was pure undiluted heaven.

When his lips left hers, to bury themselves against her throat and then the shoulder his hand had left bare by tugging down the sleeve of her nightgown, her body was so restless for his possession that she had to bite her lip to quell a desperate plea for him to simply just *take* her. But Zahir's burning eyes told Gina that he knew what she needed, what she ached for in the deepest core of her being, and he knelt in front of her, lifted her gown above her head and let it fall softly against the rug.

Lightly shaking his head, he sat back on his heels to survey her nakedness with something that looked like wonder. 'You are ravishing. I am all but stunned to silence at seeing you like this. One thing I know for sure…your beauty is beyond compare,' he uttered, low-voiced.

The tips of Gina's breasts prickled hotly, as though glanced by a burning brand. They seemed to grow hotter and harder still beneath his uninhibited hungry examination. When he put his mouth first to one and then the other to suckle Gina dragged her hands through the glossy strands of his hair greedily, to keep him there, moaning softly as the edges of his teeth nipped her. By the time he hauled her against him, she sensed his desire was at breaking point.

'Undress me,' he ordered huskily.

Almost crying with need, Gina started to carry out his order. But when he was bare-chested her busy hands grew still for a moment. Her gaze had fallen on the wound at his side, covered with a clean white dressing.

Cupping her face between hands that were warm and calloused, suggesting that he wasn't unfamiliar with hard physical graft, Zahir dismissively shook his head. 'Do not be concerned that you might hurt me. I have waited too long for this moment to let anything stop me now. You are in my blood like a fever, *rohi*. I am like a starving man at a banquet, seeing you like this. Now I will wait no more.'

The sheer beauty of his sculpted masculine physique made Gina gasp. Bare, his shoulders, torso, abdomen, hips and long well-shaped legs were pure hard muscle and bone, shielded by supple bronzed flesh, and on his chest swirled dark soft hair. Here and there were healed nicks and cuts that confirmed her opinion that he was a man who revelled in the physical challenges of life—whether it be riding his stallion through the hills and plains, as Farida had told her he liked to do, climbing high into the mountains to fearlessly confront a band of rebels, or practising sword-fighting with his guards.

But any further thoughts were stemmed as he laid her down amongst the satin pillows, passionately stroked his warm tongue into her mouth and kissed her. The deeply stirring caress had the effect of an incendiary device imploding inside her. As she reeled from the impact, molten heat like lava flowed through her bloodstream. She couldn't bear to have her body apart from his for another second.

Moving her hands from the firm flanks between his ribs and hips down to the proud, silky manhood that nudged against her belly, Gina hungrily clasped him. Zahir couldn't suppress a groan, and his answering smile was lascivious and knowing.

Paying her back in kind, he boldly prised apart her thighs, to plunge his fingers inside her moist silky heat. Her breath was all but punched out of her lungs for a moment, and dizzyingly she voraciously welcomed the bruising urgency of their mouths, teeth and tongues as his deeply rhythmic exploration took her higher and higher, winding her so tight that she almost couldn't bear it.

When her violent release came she collapsed, shuddering beneath him, emotion swamping her like an unstoppable tide. Hot, helpless tears streamed down her face, and Zahir gathered her into his arms. As he held her his lips rained kisses on her mouth, cheeks and unbound hair, until the tearful spasms slowly died away. 'It is all right. There is nothing to fear any more, my angel. I am here with you, and I will hold you and keep you safe all night.'

Hiccoughing, Gina laid her head against the warm silky hair on his chest and sighed. Through the weave of the fabric tent walls the dance of bright flame from the fire outside gradually dimmed. Inside, here in Zahir's strong arms, she realised she'd never felt safer. An intense feeling of calm suddenly came over her. The spectre of the man who had sought to abduct her faded away. He wouldn't haunt her dreams any more—not tonight at least.

Her hand drifted idly down over Zahir's flat taut abdomen, then lower still. If she'd thought that her desire had been spent in that wildly emotional release just now, she realised how wrong she'd been. It had merely been simmering, and just the touch of her lover's warm hard flesh would stir it into flame again.

Clasping her head, Zahir stared down soulfully into her eyes. Silently she transmitted her emphatic answer to the question she saw there. Reaching into a hidden pocket of his discarded robe, he sheathed himself with the protection he retrieved, then, returning to Gina's waiting arms, swept her down onto the pillows again.

Joyfully, her spirits soaring, she welcomed him inside her. His thrusts were strong, deeply possessive, and they took her body, mind and spirit into another realm. His demanding masculine possession made her ache even more to have him with her always. She almost cried again when she was reminded he couldn't be...

As soon as he entered her scalding satin heat, Zahir remembered vividly the first time he had taken this woman—remembered how their passionate joining had spun his whole world into another orbit and how it had left him reeling for days, months, *years* afterwards. That world was spinning into another sphere now. It was as though they had never been apart.

With her golden hair spread out on the silken scarlet pillow behind her, her lovely face and extraordinarily crystal blue eyes dazzling him more than the finest gemstones to be found anywhere, he jealously vowed he would never let her go again.

His heart was full and hot as he thrust deeper and harder. The emotions that flooded him were overwhelming, and so was the pleasure. There was not one other woman he had ever experienced this kind of incredible connection with... only Gina.

Her long slender legs anchored themselves round his middle, and he held back the almost overpowering temptation to just let go, to simply allow the force of his great need to overflow. As his lips fastened onto a softly rounded breast and suckled hard on the rigid nipple he knew she was close to coming apart, so he waited...

Her soft moans of pleasure turned to near cries as he took her over the edge, and they filled the tent. Then and *only* then did Zahir let go and spill his seed...

'Gina...'

The sensuously husky whisper in her ear, followed by a warm kiss nuzzled at the side of her neck, woke her from the deliciously restful sleep she'd been having. It was joy unparalleled to wake up and find Zahir's arresting handsome face smiling down at her. The last time they'd been together intimately like this seemed like eons ago.

'Good morning.'

There wasn't a place on her body that didn't throb from the delights and ecstatic release of their unrestrained lovemaking, but for some reason she couldn't fathom she suddenly felt self-conscious about finding herself naked in his arms.

'Are you blushing?' he teased, gently brushing her hair back from her face.

'No... What made you think that?'

The heat that seared her cheeks made a liar of her, but Zahir was staring at her throat as if hypnotised. The breaking dawn seeping through the stunning elaborate weave of the tent clearly illuminated his shock.

'That bastard really hurt you,' he breathed.

Unable to deny it, Gina sensed her heart bump a little beneath her ribs. 'Let's not talk about that right now.'

'At least he is behind bars now, with his no good brother. No more for *them* the comfort and hospitality of family and friends. Instead they will have to get used to the very different kind of hospitality of a high-security prison—because they will both be there for a long time!'

'I don't understand, Zahir. Who is this man's brother?' She sat up, dragging the soft wool rug that had covered them up to her chest.

His expression was formidably fierce for a second. 'He is the leader of the rebels who shot me. His brother sought to avenge his incarceration by abducting my sister when he saw her in the marketplace. Yesterday evening, in front of the captain of my security forces, he confessed everything. Because you were wearing similar clothes to Farida and had your back to him he mistook you for her. You cannot know how much I regret what happened, Gina. But the fact is my sister made a bad judgement in visiting the marketplace without adequate protection. I was speechless when I found out she'd gone there with just a servant. Especially when I had already been wounded by a crazed gunman's bullet.'

'Farida's intentions were completely good. She's slowly emerging from the pain of losing her husband and wanting to live again—to do the normal, everyday things she used to do before she lost him. Don't you think that's encouraging? She told me everything felt futile before. I thought the visit was a good idea, too, and nobody could have possibly predicted what happened.'

Concerned that if he blamed his sister for the shocking incident that had occurred it might set her recovery back even more, Gina reached out to soothingly touch Zahir's hard-muscled bicep.

'Don't be angry with her. I know how much you love her.'

'It is because I love her that I fear daily for her wellbeing and safety.' He glanced away for a moment, a muscle throbbing in his temple. 'If I were to lose her I would not—I don't think I could bear the pain.'

'I understand.' Keeping her hand on his arm, Gina yearned to reassure him. 'None of us ever want to contemplate losing the people we love. But, as hard as it is to bear, we all of us have to face loss in our lives. We can't live our lives constantly fearing it, because that's no way to live for anyone. By living in fear we only make ourselves suffer more, and we forget the tremendous privilege that life is. Don't torture yourself with thoughts of something bad happening to your sister. Just believe in the good things.'

Zahir shook his head as though amazed. 'And where did you acquire this great wisdom, I would like to know?' Heaving a sigh, he looked thoughtful. 'I extracted a promise from the rebel leader last night that there would be no more violence in retaliation for his imprisonment,' he confided. 'Some of my guards will go into the hills to make sure that promise is kept. They will see that his men go home to their wives and families. I told him things would go better for him if he lets it be known that he wants this, too, and he agreed. But be assured I will be taking no more chances. The fact of the matter is that being ruler of a kingdom means that you sometimes have to make difficult decisions in the name of the greater good. In light of recent disturbing events both you and my sister will have a regular guard. No more will I trust that I can reason with men who see violence as the only way to keep their families fed and clothed. Now, as much as I desire to stay here with you for the rest of the day, my tempting, beautiful Gina, I have my work to do, and you must return to your room and rest. I will give orders for breakfast to be brought up to you.'

'But I don't *want* to stay in my room and rest, Zahir. I want to get on with the inventory.'

'And what if you feel unwell or faint again?' he challenged, a flare of irritation in his glance.

'I won't feel unwell.'

'So you are a seer now? You can foretell the future, perhaps?'

That made Gina smile. 'Of course I can't. But I do know my own constitution, and I'm more resilient than I look.'

'Resilient and determined, I'd say…and clearly extremely stubborn!'

She lifted her shoulders in a shrug. 'I'd rather be occupied doing something that interests me than having time on my hands to frighten myself with thoughts of what happened yesterday.'

'Hmm…' Zahir tipped his head to the side. 'Maybe, in that case, it *would* be better if you occupied yourself with the inventory. All right, then, I will not stop you from carrying on with it if you want to do it—but only on the proviso that you are sensible and do not overtax yourself.'

Giving her a hard warm kiss on the mouth that could have turned lingeringly seductive if he'd willed it, he ruffled her hair with a rueful grin, then got out of their makeshift bed to dress.

CHAPTER NINE

JAKE RIVERS'S door was open as Gina passed by on the way to the terrace for breakfast. It was the first morning since she'd been at the palace that her hunger was really sharp. *Lovemaking with Zahir had certainly given her an appetite.* But that changed when she saw Jake's packed suitcase, lying open on his bed.

She rapped her knuckles lightly on the door, and he called out to her to 'Come in!' in a tone that was agitated and impatient.

'Jake? What's happening? You look like you're leaving.'

He adjusted his glasses on his nose, and his glance was preoccupied as he dropped a couple of folded Hawaiian shirts on top of the already packed clothing. 'You've got it in one. That's exactly what I'm doing Gina…*leaving!*'

'Why?'

'Do you even have to *ask* after what happened to you yesterday?' He jerked his head towards her disparagingly, clearly indicating the light pink chiffon scarf she'd looped and fastened gently round her neck to hide the bruising. 'First the Sheikh gets wounded by a gunshot, then you get half strangled by some maniac in the marketplace! I'm sorry, but I value my own neck far more than any kudos I might get researching the history of that blasted jewel—a jewel which, by the way, His Highness hasn't even had the decency to show us yet, after all our hard work!'

'The man who shot His Highness and the one who dragged me from my chair in the marketplace yesterday are both in a high-security prison now. It was just a localised skirmish, and the rebels are being helped to disband now that their leader has been imprisoned—no doubt they're probably worried about being thrown into jail themselves. Presumably they've all got families to feed. So there's no need for you to abandon your work and run away.'

'And how do you *know* these guys are in prison?'

Feeling her face heat, Gina crossed her arms over her chest. 'The Sheikh told me.'

'Did he, now?' Jake's tone was scathing. 'You two are getting very *cosy*, aren't you? Thinking of presenting yourself as a candidate for his harem, are we?'

'Don't be such an idiot!'

'I'm not an idiot, Gina. I've seen the way his eyes follow you around whenever you're both in the same room. But men in his position don't have serious relationships with women like you…no matter how pretty or intelligent they are. They only want you for one thing. I heard it rumoured that there might be an arranged marriage on the cards for our Sheikh…did you know *that?*'

It was the *last* thing she wanted to be reminded of—especially after the wonder and magic of last night. Desperately trying to quell the hurt that arose inside her, Gina took a long, steadying breath in. 'Have you told His Highness that you're intent on leaving today?'

Yanking down the lid of his suitcase and fastening it shut, Jake dragged his fingers back and forth through his already dishevelled sandy-coloured hair. 'Yes. I told him last night. He was in an all-fired hurry to leave the palace with the captain of the security forces. "Tell Jamal to arrange it," he shouted as he left, clearly not caring less. Well, I spoke to Jamal, and he made the necessary arrangements to get me out of here. Needless to say I won't be travelling home first class, as I'll just jump on any flight back to the UK I can get, but I'll willingly forego that particular pleasure to be back safe on home ground again. You should come with me, Gina.'

Not wanting to rub salt into the wound by confessing she'd taken on another job for Zahir, or let Jake see that she was in no way near ready to leave Kabuyadir, she slowly approached him as he stood by the packed suitcase on the bed. Just then he looked for all the world like some distressed and homesick boarding school boy, unsure whether his parents would turn up to collect him or not at the end of term…

'I can't go home yet. I came here to do a job, and I won't leave until I complete it. Besides…' She smiled. 'I really want to see the jewel.'

'Well, good luck with that. And what about your father? How do you think he'll feel about you staying here after you've been hurt, and with such unrest in the kingdom?'

The question made her insides jolt, as if at the impact of a heavy rock dropped into a river from a great height. 'That's none of your business. The unrest here has been quelled, and I'd seriously advise you against contacting my father to tell him I got hurt. I told you he hasn't been well.'

'It's your call, of course…'

'Yes, it is.'

'Well, I suppose I'd better be off, then. I've got a ride waiting to take me to the cable car.'

'Have a safe journey. I'm sorry that your trip had to end this way. Please give my regards to everyone when you get back to work. Tell them I'll be in touch soon, with a progress report.' Leaning forward she brushed her lips lightly over the side of his jaw. This morning he was un-shaven, she noticed. It proved how rattled he was.

Grimacing at the gesture, he glanced uncomfortably away. 'Yes, well—you probably think I'm a terrible coward, don't you?'

Feeling suddenly sorry for him, Gina moved her head, indicating no. 'Only you know what's best for you, Jake. It's not up to me to make judgements.'

'For what it's worth, I think the Sheikh would be damned lucky if you were to grace his bed...*damned* lucky.' Smiling awkwardly, he dragged his hefty suitcase off the bed and left.

'I thought I might find you out here.'

Gina hadn't seen Farida all morning, so had got on with work on the inventory by herself. Now, taking a walk in the gardens to get some fresh air, she found Zahir's sister seated on the same bench in the courtyard garden where they'd first met a few days ago. Even before she reached her she had a strong inkling that the other woman's mood was low. The beautiful gardens, with their flowers, sculptures, myriad fountains and blue skies overhead, emitted tranquil-lity and calm, but Farida's sad-eyed demeanour did not.

'I'm sorry I didn't come and find you this morning, Gina. I have had a lot on my mind. How are you feeling today? You are not in any pain, I hope? If your bruises are still sore I can apply some of that salve.'

'Don't worry about that. I'm fine.' She absently touched the chiffon scarf round her neck. 'Mind if I join you?'

The other woman moved a bit further down the bench with the briefest glimmer of a smile. 'Please do.'

Out of the corner of her eye Gina saw a palace body-guard dressed in a dark *jalabiya* and traditional headgear, observing them from the mosaic tiled archway that led into a more formal garden. At the end of the hall, where her room was situated, another similarly dressed bodyguard had been stationed by the narrow window. *Zahir had clearly meant business when he'd promised that she and his sister would have protection.* Right then Gina didn't know whether she welcomed the idea or not. The presence of a bodyguard might act as an unwanted reminder of the incident in the marketplace. She didn't want to walk round glancing over her shoulder every five minutes.

'What's the matter Farida? You look sad this morning.'

Her companion sighed. 'I did a wrong thing, taking you to the marketplace yesterday. Not only did you get hurt because that man mistook you for me, but now Zahir is furious with me. I fear I have alienated him, when he is the last person in the world I want to be alienated from.'

Automatically Gina reached for one of the slim small hands folded in the lap of the black dress and squeezed it gently. 'I doubt that you could ever alienate your brother, Farida. His love for you is unconditional and devoted. If he blames anyone for what happened I think it's more likely he blames himself.'

The almond-shaped dark eyes before her widened. 'How do you know this?'

A niggle of alarm fluttered through Gina's insides. She must be more careful about revealing her opinions on the man known as His Highness. Farida had no idea that they were having an intimate relationship, that they'd met before, or that her brother had revealed certain fears to her about his sister.

She wouldn't be so indelicate as to suggest that she'd received the information from him personally. It might cut her to the quick that Zahir was happy to take her as his mistress and not his wife, but that was between the two of them and as far as Gina was concerned would remain a strictly private matter.

She retrieved her hand to run it over the blush-pink dress she had donned that morning. 'I'm just guessing, that's all—though I can clearly tell that you're the most important thing in the world to him. It can't be easy being ruler of a kingdom…being responsible for so many important decisions. That's what I meant. Your brother obviously takes his duties very seriously, and it must grieve him when things go awry.'

'It does.' The other girl's gaze was clearly examining her as she kept it trained on Gina. 'I pray I don't offend you by saying this, Gina, but I have noticed that my brother takes a particular interest in your wellbeing…not just as someone he has hired to do a professional job for him, but as someone he seems to care personally about. Yesterday, when he knew you were hurt, I could see that he was distressed— more distressed than I have seen him for a long time, I think. Am I wrong to suspect there might be something between you…something more than just a strictly professional association?'

There was nowhere to hide. As much as she wanted to be careful and diplomatic, Zahir's sister had become a friend, and Gina wanted to respond with the same open and honest approach that she had extended to her.

She grimaced a little. A small trickle of perspiration slid down between the valley of her breasts. 'I met His Highness once before…when I first came to Kabuyadir. It was three years ago, and I had been hired to make an inventory of Mrs Hussein's rare book collection. I had just heard that my mother had been taken ill and was in hospital, and I was due to fly home the next day to see her. The Husseins were having a graduation party for their nephew, and your brother ran into me in the garden. I was upset and he was kind to me. I had no clue at the time who he was.'

Glancing round, in case Zahir himself suddenly appeared, Gina sighed and then carried on. 'We had—we had an instant connection. The kind of once-in-a-lifetime thing that you read about. I'd never, ever experienced anything as strong or profound as I experienced with—with Zahir that night.' Her cheeks flushed with heat for a moment. Farida's glance was growing more and more interested.

'Anyway, we parted after I promised him I would return…just as soon as my mother had recovered. When he rang me the first time I fully intended to do just that. I could think of little else but him. But the second time he rang my mother had died.' She made a movement indicating disbelief. 'My father seemed to age overnight, and I could see that he really needed me. When I told him about Zahir he pleaded with me to stay in England, to carry on with my career and be around so that he could see me. He was worried that I was being completely rash and irresponsible in wanting to be with a man so far away…a man I barely even knew. His argument was so convincing that I questioned my own reason for wanting to go back. All kinds of doubts and fears crept in. Kabuyadir seemed like a dream then, and England harsh reality. So when I talked to Zahir on the phone I told him I wasn't coming back after all…that my father needed me since my mother had died, and wanted me to stay and pursue my career in memory of her wishes. I think it was the hardest, most distressing conversation I have ever had. Even as I said the words to him I felt my heart break at the thought I would never see him again.'

'And how did my brother receive the news that you were not coming back?' Farida's tone was hushed, considered.

'He was…' Gina flinched. 'He was very upset.'

'Three years ago our father died, too. Then Zahir became

Sheikh. I remember at the time that he seemed to turn in on himself, as if he was strictly guarding his emotions from any possibility of further hurt. I thought it was just because we had lost our parents. Now I know he must have been grieving at losing you, too, Gina. How is it that you've come back here now, three years later, to do the inventory?'

Linking her fingers, Gina breathed in the warm spicy air for a moment. 'I changed jobs. I went to work for an auction house and the palace approached it for someone to...' She coloured guiltily as she remembered not to mention the Heart of Courage—the *real* reason she'd returned to Kabuyadir. 'Someone to do an inventory of its artefacts. It was a great shock to discover that Zahir was the ruler.'

Restless suddenly, as a sea of desperately suppressed emotion threatened to rise up and engulf her, Gina pushed to her feet.

Farida did likewise, her expression concerned. 'And now?' she asked bluntly.

'What do you mean?'

'Has Zahir not discussed the two of you getting together at last?'

Embarrassed, Gina dropped her gaze to the ground. *Why did things have to be so excruciatingly difficult?* How was she supposed to tell her lover's sister that in the future all he wanted was for her to become his mistress—and after last night hadn't she already complied? As far as Zahir's long-term plans were concerned, he seemed intent on going ahead with an arranged marriage. 'No. Not as such.'

'Why not? If he cares for you, then surely that is the next step?' Throwing her hands up in obvious frustration, Farida shook her head.

Gina was astonished that the other woman seemed to accept the idea of her having a relationship with Zahir so easily. She supposed she'd been half-afraid she might think that she was aspiring way above her station. 'Your brother intends to marry for dynastic alliance, so I hear. The very idea of a more—a more loving relationship doesn't seem to feature in his thinking at all.'

'You love him?'

She'd revealed so much already. How could she deny the one truth that disturbed her every waking moment? Gina thought. 'I do.' Her steady blue-eyed gaze was un-flinching.

One minute Farida was clasping her hands in front of her chest in wonder, the next she'd thrown her arms around Gina to hug her tight. 'You love my brother—truly love him? This is the best ever news I could have heard. It is just what he needs—to have a woman who loves him only for himself, and not because of his status or wealth. It is just as the Heart of Courage prophesised—that all our family's descendants would marry only for love.'

Heart thumping, Gina stepped out of the spontaneous embrace, her distress mounting alarmingly. 'No, Farida. You mustn't assume any such thing where Zahir is con-cerned. He is his own man, and he has to make his own decisions about what he wants. Feelings on both sides have to be taken into consideration.'

'I love Zahir dearly, but it does not blind me to his faults. He is too unbending for his own good sometimes. But if he believes he can somehow subvert his destiny then he is deluding himself. He simply cannot go through with this marriage to the Emir's daughter when it is you that he loves, Gina!'

Shocked and taken aback by the assumption, Gina gasped. 'If he ever did love me he doesn't any more. He's too angry with me for deserting him. Farida, what we've discussed must stay just between us—I'm imploring you. Please don't mention any of this to your brother.'

'Don't upset yourself, my friend. I would not dare blun-
der in and tell him what's best for him…even if he needs to
hear it. Sometimes subtlety is the way. No, I will not betray
your trust in me, Gina—I promise. For now let's get back
to work on the inventory, hmm? I will do my share with
much more dedication now that I know the truth about you
and Zahir.'

Unable to keep her worry about the situation totally at
bay, Gina accompanied the other girl thoughtfully back
into the palace. Glancing behind, she noted that Farida's
well-built bodyguard moved that way, too…

He had been gone from the palace for most of the day. Zahir
and his small entourage of guards had travelled into the
city, where he'd visited his wounded bodyguard in hospital,
then gone on to see his secretary Masoud, who had been
laid low with a virus. To his relief, both men were healing
well. By the time he returned home, all Zahir really wanted
to do was take a shower, then go and find Gina.

The library was where he finally located her. In the glow
of several softly burning lamps, she was seated behind a
long table, reading. He paused for a few moments, just for
the sheer pleasure of observing her. Her beautiful eyes were
locked onto the opened pages of her book, and she absently
curled a drifting gold strand of her hair round her finger
and let it spring free again. Zahir's avid glance honed in on
the delicate pink scarf round her neck. His gut contracted
almost violently at the sight. There was no doubt that he
felt personally responsible for her horrific experience in
the marketplace, and there was a great desire in him to
somehow make it up to her for his appalling lack of care.

It hadn't been easy to think of much else but her today.
Even when he'd been conversing with his injured bodyguard
in the hospital, and then his secretary at his house, thoughts

of Gina had drifted into his mind with increasing regularity. Their lovemaking last night had lifted his spirits and definitely renewed his energy. And this morning he had deepened his resolve to be a compassionate, fair and strong ruler, like his father before him, and make his descendants proud. That meant that he would not hesitate to make tough decisions when it came to what was best for the kingdom, even if it meant sacrificing his personal happiness. But, in truth, last night had only temporarily sated his desire for Gina—a desire that seemed to be growing in its demanding intensity rather than decreasing. The erotically charged memory ensured he had not lingered overlong in the city.

'It is getting late. And yet I find you here still working.' He moved towards her with an indulgent gentle smile.

Startled, she hastily shut the book she'd been so absorbed in and shot to her feet. Her softly pale cheeks coloured prettily. 'It doesn't feel so much like work as indulging a genuine passion,' she answered.

'Still…you have surely done enough for one day, no?'

'I suppose I have.'

She started to gather up her book and some papers from the table, and Zahir couldn't help noticing that her hands shook a little. Immediately his concerned glance swept her features for signs that she'd overtaxed herself. 'Have you rested at all today?' he demanded, knowing that he sounded gruff.

'I've been absorbed in doing something I enjoy…that's as good as resting.'

'I should have left stricter instructions with the doctor and my staff to make sure that you had some proper time off today—specifically to rest in your room.'

'I'm not a child, Zahir.'

Her resentment was evident. *He liked the way she*

pouted... Her full plump lips were the perfect vehicle for a little sexy pouting, even if she wasn't aware of it.

'If you ignore your needs and carry on regardless then you are indeed like a child—who does not know the pitfalls of her own reckless behaviour.'

Gina bit back what he guessed was an irritated reply, then with her book and papers clutched to her chest made to sweep past him.

Chuckling softly, Zahir reached out to gently but firmly waylay her. 'I did not seek you out to upset you, *rohi*. I have been thinking about you all day.'

Some of the rebellion he'd seen in her flawless blue eyes ebbed away. 'Where have you been?' she asked, and her voice had a soft catch in it. 'You weren't at breakfast, lunch or dinner.'

'Are you saying that you missed me?' he taunted.

She blushed deeply.

'I went to visit the bodyguard who got injured by that foolish rebel the other day.' With provocative deliberation Zahir's fingers tipped up her chin. 'And then I went to see my secretary, Masoud. He is recovering from a virus. When he returns to the palace I very much want you to meet him. You'd like him, I think.'

The pad of his thumb pressed into her fulsome lower lip. Along with the provocative sensation of her vulnerable soft mouth beneath his thumb, the heated little gasp that feathered over him hardened him instantly.

'Will he...will he be back soon?'

'Masoud? I hope so... Maybe in another week or two.'

As much as he respected his loyal employee and friend, Zahir was in no mood to discuss him any further.

He lowered his hand to retrieve the book and papers Gina still clung onto so avidly. 'Why don't you put these down for a while, hmm?'

She released them reluctantly, and he laid them back down on the table. Then he gathered her face between his hands so that he could examine her lovely features at close quarters. The quiver that he sensed went through her reminded him of a delicate rose petal, shivering in the wind. Not able to resist the temptation of that seductive yet innocent mouth any longer, he lowered his lips to hers. The sensual meeting was like a dizzying conflagration— an explosion of feeling, need and want like no other. If a tremor had ruptured the earth right then beneath his feet, Zahir could not have felt as shaken.

His palms slid over her shoulders down to her breasts. Catching the burgeoning nipples between thumb and fore-finger, through her dress and the delicate lace bra she wore underneath, he mercilessly provoked the already rigid tips to grow harder still. With the softly velvet whimpers that sounded in his ears inflaming him, he moved his eager hands down to the seductive womanly curve of her hips, then her delightfully shaped bottom. The thin, clingy silk of her dress was hardly any barrier at all to his fevered exploration.

The scalding heat all but flooding his loins practically rendered Zahir mindless. He was a mere breath away from dragging Gina down to the conveniently long library table and taking her in the most basic, feral way when she wrenched her lips free from his and flattened her palm against his chest. His breathing a hotly ragged rasp, he stared into her languorous blue eyes in shock.

'We can't be crazy like this. Have you forgotten that there's a bodyguard outside? A bodyguard that *you* insisted follow me everywhere.'

The thought hadn't even entered his head, even though he'd passed the man in the hallway before he'd entered the library. Zahir immediately dismissed her concern with unconcealed irritation. 'So? He is trained to be discreet as well as to defend and protect.'

He would have pulled Gina back into his arms if not for the fact that she was already moving away from him. Looking as if her mind was already made up as to what she would do next, she collected the book and papers he'd lain on the table and once more held them against her chest. Her features were flushed, her clothes sexily disarranged—and so was the golden hair that threatened to tumble free from its clasp at any moment.

Inside his chest, Zahir's heart thumped in an agitated blend of frustration and pure unadulterated lust. 'Where are you going?'

She lowered her gaze. 'I'm feeling tired all of a sudden. You're right…I think I should go and rest now.'

'You cannot be serious?' He stared at her as if she'd taken leave of her senses. Did she have any idea how much *pain* he was in right now? And he wasn't referring to the flesh wounds he'd received, either.

'I'm not pretending. I really *am* tired.'

'You would rather sleep than stay and finish what we started? Didn't you enjoy our lovemaking last night?'

Gina went very still for a moment. 'Of course I did. It was incredible. But I'm trying to be respectful—to you and to myself. There's a time and a place for everything, and… like I said…there's a bodyguard outside.'

Dragging his fingers through his long unbound hair, Zahir could hardly contain his mounting frustration. 'If you are worried that we might be overheard, then we can retire to my quarters instead.'

'Not tonight, Zahir. I'm not trying to deliberately frustrate you, but it's been a tiring day and I *am* going back to my rooms now. I'll see you in the morning. Goodnight.'

Her head held high, and more regal than any princess

he had ever met, Gina walked past him and out of the
room. Shaking his head in dazed disbelief, Zahir kicked a
nearby chair and sent it skidding noisily across the marble
floor. Instantly he heard the running footsteps of the alert
guard race towards him from outside in the corridor, and
vehemently cursed under his breath.

CHAPTER TEN

INSTEAD of seeking out the relaxing steam of the *hamam* bath, followed by a massage, Zahir had stormed back to his quarters the night before, and immersed himself in the longest cold shower known to man. Afterwards he'd turned and tossed as though he were in the grip of a fever, and had barely slept a wink. Gina's unexpected rejection of his amorous attentions in the library had left him feeling aggrieved, ill-treated and sore.

How dared she rebuff him like that? Reminding him that the bodyguard he'd instructed to watch over her waited outside had been just an excuse. Why did she now seem wary of the passion that erupted between them whenever they were together? She was a young, vibrant woman, with needs just like any other woman, and Zahir was a fit and healthy male with a strong libido. Why couldn't she simply allow herself to enjoy fully the opportunity for them to be together and receive the sensual pleasure that he was more than willing to provide? Was she afraid that he would just use her and forgo all respect for her?

Furious at the fact she'd left him frustrated, and unwilling to explore the unsettling thought that his feelings for her might run a little deeper than having her as a convenient bedmate to assuage his lust, Zahir set out early that next morning to travel with a small entourage into the neighbouring kingdom of Kajistan. It was a day and a half's journey, so he'd be gone for at least three days. *Three days for Gina to reflect on what a mistake she'd made in so foolishly turning him down.* At least that was his hope.

He determinedly cast the irksome thought aside. He was making the journey to Kajistan—because after the recent distasteful events with the rebels—Kabuyadir needed to make an outward demonstration of stability. How better to achieve that than by his marrying, and aligning the ruling dynasty with another great house? A cause for celebration would help to reassure everyone.

And so it had come to him, in the sleepless early hours of the morning, that perhaps it was time to run a more serious gaze over the Emir's marriageable daughter...

'Gina! Gina, I have to talk to you.'

Lost in a world of her own in the library yet again—she'd gone there in search of peace and consolation after a torturous sleepless night during which her thoughts had been consumed with Zahir—Gina glanced up in surprise to find the Sheikh's pretty sister bearing down on her, her expression distressed.

'Is something wrong?' *She prayed it didn't concern Zahir.*

She'd seen the look of hurt and frustration on his face last night, when she'd declined his suggestion of going to bed with him, but she'd honestly been emotionally drained after the incident in the marketplace, and had needed to retreat and lick her wounds a little. She also didn't want him to think she would sleep with him at the drop of a hat just because of their night together in the Bedouin tent.

Perhaps they both needed some space and time to reflect and assess the situation? But right then the idea that some harm might have come to him filled her with icy dread.

'Zahir left the palace early this morning to travel to Kajistan.'

'Kajistan?'

'Remember I told you about the Emir and his daughter?' Farida dropped down into the chair across the table from her a little breathlessly. 'He's gone there to consolidate his marriage plans.'

A silent hurt scream echoed despairingly round the chambers of Gina's heart. Keeping her hand on the opened yellowed leaf of the journal she'd been studying, she fought hard to conceal her distress, but knew she failed miserably.

'He has?' She knew she looked as devastated as she felt.

Farida plucked her hand from the book and held it warmly. 'We can't let him ruin his life like this, Gina—we just can't! When he returns you must tell him that you love him.'

'No.' She firmly tugged her hand free. 'He's made his decision about what he wants from a relationship, Farida, and it's not a woman who loves him. If making your dynasty stronger by aligning himself with the emirate of Kajistan is what's important to him, then so be it.'

'So be it? Have you lost your mind, Gina? Don't you believe in fighting for the man you love?'

'I won't fight for a man who doesn't love *me,* Farida… What would be the point? I might keep him for a while, as long as he desires me, but what happens when he finds somebody else he likes more? I'd be utterly devastated. If Zahir doesn't believe in love, then I can't *make* him believe in it.'

'So you'd rather just stand by and let him marry the dull, boring daughter of the Emir of Kajistan?'

'I didn't say I'd rather do that.'

Despondent, Gina sighed with private terror. Now she regretted abandoning their lovemaking in the library last night. How terrible if her hurt pride had stood in the way of allowing Zahir to be close to her once more. Especially if after his return from Kajistan it turned out to be the last opportunity she'd ever had!

'Have you completely forgotten the prophecy of the Heart of Courage? The prophecy that states every descendant of the house of Kazeem Khan will marry for love?'

The other woman's beautiful almond eyes were imploring. Taking a deep breath before she replied, Gina knew she had to be honest about something at last—something that had seriously been troubling her since she'd been asked to keep it secret. 'Farida...I didn't come here purely to do the inventory. The auction house I work for in London was approached by your brother to corroborate the research and provenance of the Heart of Courage. He plans to sell it, we were told...because he thinks of it as a curse on his family.'

'Are you serious?'

'I'm afraid so.'

'I have heard him talk about it as a curse before, but I had no idea that he planned to sell it...to be rid of it for good. In truth, I am utterly shocked to hear this.'

'I'm so sorry I've had to be the bearer of such disturbing news. It's because your parents died so close to each other and then you lost your beloved husband in the accident. Zahir thinks that in marrying for love you were cursed—not blessed by the prophecy associated with the jewel.'

'His mind must have slipped into temporary madness!' The other girl's skin turned abnormally pale for a few moments. 'How could he contemplate selling such an important piece of our family's history? He is just scared, that's all...scared that if he should fall in love that love would be ripped away by some awful tragedy and he would never get over it. I have always considered my brother to be one of the bravest men I know, but now I see that when it comes to one of the most important things of all in life he is a coward.'

Gina wanted to respond—but how? Words seemed terribly inadequate right then. But now she felt as if she understood why Zahir would seek an arranged marriage rather than a love-match.

Her hand idly but carefully turned over a couple of the journal pages in front of her. Inside her a little flame of hope lit and wouldn't be doused. 'For what it's worth, Farida, I was captured by the jewel and its wonderful prophecy from the moment I heard about it. It's practically all I can think about. And I may have an idea,' she said, indicating the book on the table.

'What do you have there?'

'It's an old family journal I found. It must be a couple of hundred years old at least. The only problem is my knowledge of your language is nowhere near good enough to understand it. I can make out some odd words and phrases, but that's all.'

'Why don't I help you?' Zahir's sister leapt up from her seat to move round the table and join her. 'I don't think I've ever seen this.' Her fingers stroked the intricately embroidered cover patterned with silk flowers in wonder. 'Where did you find it?'

Gina flushed guiltily. 'It was tucked away on one of the higher bookshelves. When I spotted it I guessed it must be a personal record of some kind. To tell you the truth I've been looking for evidence of marriages in the dynasty that have fulfilled the prophecy and continued happily right up until the end.'

After perusing the contents with their beautifully

scripted writing for a few moments, Farida glanced back at her companion with excitement brimming in her eyes. 'This is my great-great-grandmother's journal, and in it she mentions the Heart of Courage! She's bound to have mentioned her own marriage at least, and if it was happy or not.'

Daring to stay with the hope that had been ignited inside her, Gina silently shook her head in wonder, even as the edges of her teeth clamped down anxiously on her lip…

For three years Gina had been bereft of Zahir's presence. But now, having seen him again, and knowing for certain that she had never stopped loving him and never would, the three days of his absence from the palace was like being slowly tortured.

Oh, she filled her days well enough with the job of the inventory, and Farida had been the kindest and best hostess and friend…but every cell in her body *ached* interminably to see Zahir again, and hopefully get the chance to show him just how much she cared. The idea of him returning with news of his upcoming wedding was like an approaching violent storm about to tear down her house, but Gina told herself she would *not* leave Kabuyadir without expressly telling him exactly how she felt once and for all. She *would* fight for the man she loved, and if after that he still rejected her then she would just have to accept that it wasn't her destiny to be with him after all.

Zahir was glad to finally arrive back at the palace. The sight of the turrets blazing like molten gold in the afternoon sun filled his heart with both pride and joy. It was good to be home. He'd spent most of the journey there and back again from Kajistan consumed with concern about Gina and his sister. Having given instructions that their personal bodyguards were to be extra-vigilant and stay close to them at all times, as well as posting extra guards round the palace and in the watchtower, he was still not totally reassured they were safe.

The uprising might have been quelled with the imprisonment of the rebel leader and his equally hot-headed brother, but after the incident Gina had suffered in the marketplace he knew there was no such thing as being *too* careful. On his way to Kajistan he had wrestled painfully with the wisdom of what he intended. He had almost turned back... *almost*.

'Zahir!' Farida ran towards him as he strode down the hallway towards his personal quarters. She hugged him hard, then stood back to survey him. She appeared a little nervous, he thought, and his brow furrowed in concern. 'I'm so glad you're back,' she said.

'All is well here?'

'Yes, everything's fine—absolutely fine. How was your trip?'

Her small hands twisted restlessly in front of her black silk dress, prompting a quizzical smile from Zahir. 'You are sure?'

'Perfectly sure.'

'Well, my trip was fine, too. The Emir's hospitality was second to none, as usual.'

'And what of his daughter?'

'She was...' He concentrated hard for a moment on how much to tell. 'She was very well.'

Suddenly brother and sister were like two awkward strangers, trying to make conversation at a party neither had wanted to attend. Zahir regretted that, but there would be time enough to make amends. Right now he was anxious to get out of his travelling clothes and take a reviving shower. But there was one subject he had to touch upon before he left.

'And Gina…how is she?'

Farida's answering smile was broad. 'She's good. We've been working hard on the inventory. She's upstairs in one of the galleries, surrounded by books and papers, researching the history of a pair of ancient urns from Persia—you know the ones I mean?'

She saw by his raised eyebrows that he did.

'She absolutely loves the work. It's a joy to spend time with her. I've learned so much about our own family's heritage through Gina. By the way—I've arranged a special dinner tonight for your return, so we can all convene then and hear each other's news.'

'That was thoughtful of you. Right now I would like to shake off the dust of my travels, have a shower and change into some fresh clothes. I will see you this evening at dinner.' Briefly Zahir touched the side of her face, then continued on down the long corridor to his private domain.

Not hearing the soft tread on the carpeted hall floor, Gina chewed thoughtfully on her pencil as she perused the delicate urns on the plinth in front of her. She had been trying to date them. Her training and intuition led her towards believing they were two of the finest examples of some of the earliest glazed pottery in the world—probably from the Achaemenian era of the Persian Empire, she thought. Sitting back on her heels, she silently admired their incredible artistry—particularly the figures of some archers, with their still dazzling gold and silver swords.

'The inventory is keeping you very busy, I see. I fear I am working you too hard, Dr Collins.'

The gently teasing warm male voice from behind made Gina grow still. Slowly, she turned, and the imposing sight of Zahir dressed in his fine robes, dark hair shining fiercely even in the half-light of the evening, and his eyes glinting in mocking merriment, made her heart race madly. He was home. *At last...*she thought feverishly.

Removing the pencil she'd been absently chewing, she smiled helplessly shy—because all of a sudden it was as if she was meeting him for the first time. 'Like I told you before...it's not like work when it's a genuine passion. Did you have a good trip to Kajistan?'

On the last word Gina lowered her gaze, because she didn't really want to know if his trip had been good if 'good' meant that he'd become officially engaged to the Emir's daughter.

'If you are asking if I had a safe and uneventful journey, then the answer to that question is yes. As for the hospitality of the Emir—that lived up to its famously high standard, as always, and did not disappoint.'

Making a slow, measured approach, Zahir was suddenly in front of her. His leather boots were buffed to a mirror-shine, she noticed, and just as her eager glance travelled upwards to examine the rest of him he dropped down to his haunches, so that their gazes were level. The fine calf leather of his boots creaked a little as he lowered himself, and the arousing scents of agarwood and sandalwood made a potent assault against senses that were already under siege.

It was all Gina could do to keep her fingers laced together in her lap and not reach out to touch him.

'I'm glad that you're back safe,' she said softly.

'I confess it is good to be home again. You have a pencil

smudge at the corner of your mouth. Here…' He leaned forward and gently rubbed at it.

Gina all but held her breath. 'It's a bad habit of mine, I'm afraid,' she murmured. 'Chewing the end of pencils, I mean.'

Smiling into her eyes, Zahir withdrew again. 'Those urns were two of my father's favourite pieces,' he commented, nodding his head towards them.

'Were they? Your father must have had impeccable taste, then, as well as being a bit of a historian. *Was* he interested in history?'

'He was, as a matter of fact. How could he not be when he lived amongst so many incredible historical treasures in this palace?'

'What was he like? Will you tell me?' Again Gina almost held her breath. As yet he had never shared with her any personal details of his family, or how the loss of his parents—particularly his father—had affected him. She knew how a son's relationship with his father and the example he'd had from his first and most important male role model shaped their future.

'He was definitely the authority figure in our home, but he was never cruel or unfair. He loved us all very much and showed it daily. He was also revered by our people. Trust me…' he grimaced ruefully 'he was a very hard act to follow. It devastated me when he died not very long after my mother. Sometimes I imagine I can still hear the deep rumble of his laughter, or the firmness of his voice instructing the guards echoing round the palace walls. Anyway… he is gone now.'

Gina said softly, 'You must miss him very much, Zahir.'

'Every day.' He quickly shielded the emotion that she had briefly detected in his tone. 'I came to find you not just to say hello, but to inform you—at my sister's request—that dinner will be served in the dining room in about one hour. See how she makes me useful? Perhaps you should finish what you're doing and go and get ready? Farida tells me it is a special meal to welcome me home.'

'Of course… I completely forgot the time.' Getting herself ready to stand, she was taken by surprise when Zahir stood up first, then reached out his hand to help her. He held on to her for several long seconds as his dark eyes roamed her face.

'I never knew that just three days away from the people I care about could seem like a lifetime, but it did…' His voice was suddenly pitched sensually low. 'It did.'

Desperate to ask him what he meant by 'the people I care about', Gina nevertheless remained silent. Was he including her in that exclusive little group? If so, what about his engagement to the Emir's daughter? It was so frustrating not to know what he intended. Didn't he realise it was all but *killing* her to imagine him married to someone else?

'I'd better go and get ready for dinner. I know Farida's been busy organising the menu with the kitchen staff all day,' she murmured.

'Do you have anything else in *this* colour?' Zahir nodded his head towards her silky aquamarine kaftan. 'If you have, I would like you to wear it. It complements your eyes and reminds me of a too rare glimpse of the sea. I like it very much.'

It wasn't exactly easy to mentally assess her wardrobe right then, when he'd made such a surprisingly personal request, but Gina managed a shrug and answered, 'I think I might have something else in the colour. I'll check when I go back to my rooms.'

'Good. I will look forward to seeing you at dinner, then.'

He was walking back down the corridor, his long robes swirling round his booted calves, before she could even think to move and gather up her papers from the carpeted floor...

They were dining in a room Gina had not had the privilege of seeing before, but once seen it would be hard to forget. Above the long burnished table at which they sat was a vaulted ceiling, with a stunning circular dome made up of several different sections of vividly coloured glass. On the walls were lavishly painted murals of scenes depicting days of a powerful empire long gone, and a theme of arabesque patterning could be seen throughout, inlaid to particularly stunning effect in the marble floor. The space was lit tonight by softly glowing candles encased in lanterns—both on the walls and on the beautifully laid table. With the scent of spices and incense hanging in the air, it was like walking into a magical scene from the country's magnificent past.

After they'd washed their hands in a ritualistic vessel filled with warm water, they sat in silence as the servants passed various aromatic dishes of food from guest to guest.

Relieved to find it was just to be the three of them tonight, Gina tried hard to relax—but it wasn't easy with Zahir sitting opposite her, his darkly hypnotic glance frequently locking with hers and making her insides jump.

Of the three of them, it was Farida who seemed most at ease. Tonight her pretty face was literally glowing with pleasure at having her brother safely home again.

The servants departed—including Jamal, at Zahir's express request—and Farida raised her glass of fruit juice in a toast. 'To Zahir, in honour of your safe return from Kajistan after what has been a difficult time for us all...and for your steadfast, dedicated and wise rule of the kingdom. Our father would have been more than proud.'

He seemed taken aback. Was that a flush of hot colour beneath his bronzed skin? 'I have only ever wanted to honour his great memory by doing justice to his faith in me,' he murmured. 'And if I can do that even in a small way I should be very glad.'

'To Zahir.' Gina flushed as the handsome recipient of the toast glanced her way. *Should she have said Your Highness, instead of addressing him so personally?* But he was smiling, and for a moment she breathed a little easier.

'Thank you, my sister…and you also, Gina. Like I said earlier, I am very glad to be home again. I've returned with some important news.'

Gina's reprieve from anxiety was not yet over. Her insides tightened painfully. Was this where he announced that he was officially engaged to the Emir's daughter? If so, was she willing to remain in Kabuyadir as his mistress, knowing that he would never wholly be hers? Returning her glass to the table, she nervously brushed an imaginary piece of lint from the long sleeve of the aquamarine top that matched her long silk skirt.

Her expression equally concerned, Farida's voice was falsely bright. 'Perhaps we should enjoy our meal before you tell us your news, Zahir?'

He frowned. 'It is most unlike you not to want to hear my news straight away, Farida.' Narrowing his gaze, he silently assessed her for a moment. 'I think you must have undergone a serious change of character while I've been gone if that is the case.'

'Not at all. I have simply been much more at peace with Gina here to keep me company. I've very much enjoyed working alongside her on the inventory. It has really helped me find some purpose at last. These things have occupied my time and my mind much more than idle speculation about what news you might bring from Kajistan.'

'So to ponder on the news I bring from that place is "idle speculation"?' He grinned. 'You really know how to deflate a man's ego, my sister! Well, whatever else is happening, it is very good to learn that you are in a much better place and that your spirits have lifted. Now—regardless—I will tell all.'

With her tummy full of fluttering butterflies, Gina held onto her drinking glass as though it was an anchor in wildly stormy seas. Again, her appetite for any sustenance other than Zahir's drugging, passionate kisses fled.

'As you know, I had talked about the possibility of marriage with the Emir's daughter.'

'And I believe I told you I did not think that was such a good idea,' the girl at Gina's side piped up accusingly.

At the side of Zahir's bronzed cheekbone a muscle ticked irritably. 'As always, sister, your views are never kept hidden from me. In a strange sort of way I suppose I should appreciate it that you care enough to share them with me.'

The corners of his mouth were duelling with a smile again, and Gina wondered how that was possible when he was just about to break her heart into a million shattered pieces.

'All right, Zahir. Just put us out of our misery and get on with it, will you?'

Now his sister's voice was petulant. In answer, Zahir wiped his hands on his fine linen napkin, then let it drop back down onto the table again. 'My news is that I will *not* be getting engaged to the Emir's daughter after all.'

'You won't? I mean, you're not?' Farida's brown eyes were twin mirrors of stunned surprise.

Meanwhile, after the unbearable tension of waiting for his announcement, Gina almost crumpled with relief.

With a heartfelt sigh, Zahir studied both girls. 'The most surprising thing happened. I learned that the Emir does not want to relegate his beloved only daughter to a love-less marriage—no matter how influential or beneficial. It seems he is much influenced by the legend attached to our infamous family jewel, and is breaking with his family's tradition by now believing that she should only marry a man who adores her. Also, he does not believe it would be a good thing for a descendant of my father to go against the prophecy and marry merely for convenience or dynas-tic alliance. He admitted he fears possible "supernatural" repercussions if I were to go against it. So...' an intriguing but puzzling little half-smile played about his lips '...it seems there will be no dynastic marriage to bring our two powerful kingdoms together after all.'

'That's wonderful!'

At her brother's reproving glance Farida blushed, then quickly tried to play down her obvious delight.

'I don't mean it's wonderful that our kingdoms will not benefit from a marriage between our houses. I just mean that it's great that the Emir believes his daughter should only marry a man who adores her. I am happy for her... that's what I meant. Underneath her dull exterior she's a sweet girl, and deserves to be in love.'

'You are happy for her, are you? What about your poor brother?' Zahir's silky dark eyes belied his reprimanding tone. They were positively twinkling...

'Perhaps...perhaps you could revise your opinion about the jewel and open your mind to the possibility of being with someone that *you* adore as well, Zahir? It's not outside the bounds of feasibility that a woman—a *lovely* woman—might fall in love with you.'

His powerful shoulders lifted in what might have been a resigned shrug. 'Maybe… It is definitely a consideration.' The smile now touching his lips grew wider. 'In fact, it would not be a lie to admit that I am coming round to believing that perhaps it *is* completely the right thing to do after all…to marry a woman I adore and cherish.'

As he finished speaking his dark chocolate gaze was drawn to Gina. And as her hungry eyes were magnetised by his she felt them well helplessly with tears.

'Gina and I found our great-great-grandmother's journal, and in it she mentions the Heart of Courage,' Farida related eagerly. 'She affirms that she had total belief in the truth of the prophecy because *all* our ancestors before her had enjoyed very happy, successful marriages, and most of them died of natural causes. There was no mention of any terrible tragedies being visited upon them.' She took a deep breath, and her smile was wistful and sad for a moment. 'It was a terrible blow for me to lose Azhar…but I will not rail at the heavens for it. I think that would be sheer arrogance— because clearly I do not know the mind of the Divine, or for what reason Azhar was taken from me so young. But just because that happened to me, Zahir, it does not mean that it will happen to *you*. You mustn't spend your whole life dreading such a thing. As for our parents—we already knew that Father had a weak heart. It simply gave way because Mother died. It was his time…'

Reaching across the table, Zahir tenderly covered his sister's small hand with his own much larger one. 'You are very brave, Farida… I am truly blessed to have such a one as you as my sister. I know Azhar was the love of your life, but perhaps, given time, you might open your heart to the possibility of loving again? You are young yet, and have too much to offer to be alone.'

Relaxing back in his chair, he almost immediately moved

his attention to Gina again. His intense examination of her gave her goosebumps. It made the hope rising inside her almost bubble over—just as though she had imbibed too much champagne. She felt quite heady with joy. Yet an old fear that she might not get her heart's desire after all dampened it down a little. *Whoever heard of a boring academic marrying the handsomest Sheikh in the world?* it mocked.

Determined to ignore it, she pulled her glance determinedly away from the strong, handsome face at the opposite side of the table, to contemplate the delicious selection of food on her plate instead.

'You are hungry, Gina?'

Zahir's tone was teasing but she found she didn't mind it...didn't mind it at all. 'I am as a matter of fact,' she admitted shyly.

'Then, seeing as I do not want to be responsible for my treasured guest fainting with hunger, please go ahead and eat. You too, Farida.'

The grin hijacking his wonderful features elevated his handsome face to the most stunning male visage Gina had ever seen, and for a few moments it was all but impossible for her to look anywhere else.

'Let us enjoy this wonderful feast that my sister has organised for us,' he continued. 'There will be plenty of time for conversation afterwards.'

'A thousand apologies, Your Highness.' The twin doors opened abruptly, and Jamal appeared. He went straight up to Zahir.

'What is it?'

'A telephone call from the house of Masoud.'

The rest of the servant's explanation was in their own language, and both Gina and Farida tensed as Zahir stood up from the table and threw down his napkin. As he surveyed them, his dark eyes were fever-bright. Was that *fear* she saw reflected there? Gina thought anxiously.

'I have to go out, I'm afraid,' he said. 'My secretary Masoud has taken a sudden turn for the worse. Please try and enjoy your food without me, and I will see you both later.' Turning to Jamal, he laid his hand on the other man's shoulder. 'I am charging you to look after my sister and my guest,' he said clearly.

As he swept towards the door, his handsome profile grimly resolute, Gina shot up from her seat and rushed round the table towards him. 'Zahir!' She stopped him in his tracks, and for a jittery moment wondered at her own audacity.

'What's wrong?' he asked, not without a hint of impatience.

'Let me go with you.'

'That is out of the question.'

'Please… I've heard in your voice how highly you regard Masoud, and I thought—I thought I might be able to be of some help.'

'Help? How? A medical doctor is what I need right now—not an expert in antiquities!'

Ignoring the barbed retort, Gina pressed on. 'I don't like the thought of you keeping a lonely vigil. At least if I was there you'd have someone to share your thoughts and concerns with. Please, won't you change your mind and let me go with you?'

'No. I want you to stay here with Farida. Like I said before, I will see you both later.' And with that he swept through the double doors and was gone.

CHAPTER ELEVEN

It had been a long night—a night during which his loyal secretary and friend Masoud had literally been fighting for his life.

The medical staff at the small exclusive hospital that Zahir had had him flown to by helicopter had worked like Trojans to keep him alive. Earlier that day another virus had taken hold of him, leaving him dangerously ill, but in the early hours of the morning the senior doctor in charge had at last given him the all-clear, and informed Zahir that the man was over the worst. Only the days to come would tell whether he had enough strength left in his compromised immune system to pull through completely.

Grey-faced and anxious, Zahir returned to the palace. In his room he collapsed on the bed, and stared up at the gently whirring blades of the ceiling fan. Like his friend Amir, Masoud had been to school with him. He, too, was like a brother. To see his gaunt face and black eyes staring blankly up at him from a hospital bed, his body wired up to countless tubes and drips, had left him in a state of mounting fear and despair. *Was he to lose yet another person he cared about?*

He had no doubt he was being tested by Allah—although it felt more as if he was being mocked. Just when he'd decided to give love a chance, he had again been shown how precarious his future with Gina might be if he should lose her. He was strong, but not *that* strong. If she should die young—either by some dreadful accident or through an illness of some kind—he honestly didn't think he could bear it. With his heart and mind in turmoil, Zahir shut his eyes and prayed harder than he had ever prayed before…

It seemed as though Zahir had retreated from her in every possible way. Gina had got over the abrupt way he'd told her that he needed a medical doctor, not an antiquities expert, telling herself it was because he'd been so distressed on hearing the news about Masoud. He had been so curt— and it had wounded her when he'd so brutally dismissed her offer of help.

More troubling behaviour was to come.

The morning after he'd rushed to Masoud, Gina saw him on the way to his rooms. His handsome, unlined face was haggard.

'Zahir.' She hurried after him. It appeared that he was reluctant to stop even for a moment to talk to her.

'What is it?' he asked wearily, rubbing his hand across his eyes.

Her heart knocked hard against her ribs. 'How is Masoud?'

'Right now it is touch and go, so I am told. To speak the truth, I don't really want to discuss it. All I will say is that the next few days are critical. If you need anything, talk to Farida or Jamal, will you?'

'I don't want to annoy you, Zahir, but perhaps the next time you go to the hospital I *could* go with you? I know I can't make your friend better, but I could be a support and someone to turn to for you, instead of you sitting there alone worrying about him.'

'To be frank, your presence would be an unnecessary

distraction rather than a support. Right now I need to focus on what has to be done for my friend—not be fussed over by a woman like some needy child!'

Biting back a hurt retort, Gina felt her face burn at having her offer of help again so bluntly refused. 'Well…' She twisted her hands in front of her and shrugged. 'If you change your mind at any time I just want you to know that I'll be here for you…that's all.'

'Hmm…' His distant gaze withdrew from her even before he turned and continued down the corridor.

Frozen into a statue, Gina stood staring after him.

Every time Zahir came into contact with her after that morning he deliberately kept their exchanges to the minimum, then made himself absent as soon as possible. After the high hopes of his homecoming dinner, it was a painful knock-back.

He was travelling back and forth to the hospital to visit Masoud on a regular basis. One day the news was good, the next not so good. Frequently his expression bordered on the haunted.

Gina had tried to reach him with words, with warmth, with an understanding look, but his self-protective shutters had definitely slammed down as hard as a heavy portcullis, and nothing seemed to make an impact. She had no choice but to bide her time. Even now, when he seemed so distant and the possibility of them being together seemed ever more remote and impossible, she vowed she would not give up on her love for him.

Masoud becoming ill had shaken him to his core—she knew that. She also knew that he feared losing his friend as he had lost his parents and then his brother-in-law. He feared the pain that it would bring. Farida's plea that he should not spend his life dreading the loss of those he loved had apparently been forgotten.

'Do not despair,' the other woman had consoled her. 'Masoud's health will return, and so will Zahir's belief in love.'

Not allowing herself too much time in which to speculate on what would happen if Masoud *didn't* recover, Gina kept her gloomy thoughts at bay by working on the inventory. But underlying everything she did was her hope and prayer that Zahir would come back to himself and *her* soon.

Five nights after Zahir had left his homecoming dinner to rush off to his friend's bedside, they learned that Masoud was emerging from the nightmare of his illness with flying colours. The medical staff had removed the drips, and he had even had his first taste of solid food for days. Zahir was in much higher spirits, even seeking Gina out in one of the galleries where she was working to speak with her.

'I am off to the hospital again. I feel like I'm taking up residence there, if you want to know the truth.'

His smile still looked tired, Gina thought as she studied him, but the haunted expression was thankfully gone. She was very moved that he would be so dedicated to the care of a friend that he would put him before everything else... even duty...yet inside she was wrestling with the agonising idea that he didn't want to be with her at all. That she was, as he had said, just an *unnecessary distraction*.

'When I return later tonight I want to see you,' he declared. 'I want to tell you things—' He broke off to arch a rueful dark eyebrow. 'I have not been the best host or the kindest and most understanding friend to you in the past few days, Gina... But I promise I will make it up to you.'

'You don't owe me anything, Zahir—honestly. I'm just very glad that your friend is getting better and that consequently you won't be so worried.'

'Yet still I feel I have neglected you.'

'I assure you, you have not. Like you, I'm not "some needy child" who needs constant attention or fussing over. At the end of the day I merely came here to do a job. When that job is ended I'll go back home again, and you won't have to give me another thought.' Her throat swelled and tightened as she finished speaking, and hot, despairing tears weren't far away.

'You think I would never give you another thought if you should return home?' The tanned brow furrowed in not just concern, but confusion and annoyance, too. 'Have I been so remiss in my care of you that you would leave and dismiss me as if my feelings were of no account whatsoever?' he demanded.

'Forget what I said, Zahir.' Having great difficulty in containing her spiralling emotions, Gina forced a smile to her lips. 'You need to focus on your friend, and I understand that—I really do. When you return I'll still be here, working on the inventory. I promise.'

Not looking entirely convinced, nonetheless Zahir briefly gathered her hand in his, then raised it to his lips to deliver a tender kiss across the fine skin of her knuckles. His eyes watched her carefully as he did so, almost as if he expected her to bolt like a rabbit. 'I pray that will be so, *rohi*.' His rich voice was husky and warm with feeling. 'When I return I will come straight away to see you no matter what the time is.'

Almost faint with the mixture of relief and hope that had swirled through her at his words, after he had gone Gina took some time out from doing the inventory with Farida. She simply went to her rooms to try and calm the nervous excitement that had suddenly turned her brain to mush and her limbs to sponge...

'You are still up? I was hoping you would be.'

Farida had gone to bed quite a while ago, he'd learned,

and at last…*at last* Zahir had an opportunity to have Gina to himself. *If* she was still awake, that was. He'd knocked on her door, half expecting her to be fast asleep in bed. It was, after all, past midnight. But she'd answered his knock almost immediately, her shy glance lit up by an equally unsure smile.

'I waited for you. You said you wanted to tell me things.'

'I did, didn't I?'

'How was Masoud today?' she asked, her expression concerned but wary.

Breathing out a long sigh, Zahir nodded his head. 'He has made a miraculous recovery, and is looking even better than before. Two or three more days in hospital to recuperate and he will be home again. Take a walk with me, will you?'

'A walk where?'

'Not very far.'

They moved slowly down the lamp-lit corridor and both fell silent. Dressed in a soft white tunic and skirt, her bright hair arranged behind her head with a pretty floral clasp, the woman at Zahir's side made his heart soar just looking at her. But it had taken a ruler wiser than he—a ruler who *did* listen to his heart—to make him finally acknowledge the depth and breadth of his feelings. Masoud's illness had set his hopes back for a while, Zahir silently admitted, but only because he'd feared his friend might not survive. Now he realised that even if he had *not* life would go on, *Zahir* would go on, and his great hope now was that he would do so with Gina by his side.

'I want to show you something.'

He caught her by the hand, then pushed open a door to the side of him. The small salon was barely furnished, but that was for a good reason. Inside there was a single glowing lamp, and on the wall a stunning landscape of the desert. The painting had been one of his mother's own works. She'd loved to paint, and her favourite subject had been the diversity and beauty of this incredible land they lived in. Beneath the picture was a beechwood cabinet with a clear glass top, so that whatever was laid inside there could be viewed to its best advantage. It was the reason there was so little else in the room—so nothing could detract from its incredible beauty and presence.

Placing his hand gently at the small of her back, Zahir urged Gina towards it. 'You have been so patient, *rohi*, and this is your reward. You are looking upon the Heart of Courage.'

The jewel seemed especially lovely tonight, as it lay on its bed of black velvet, he mused. With a buttery-yellow gold chain, the stunning pendant was made up of a circle of rubies and sapphires—and at its centre, dazzling the eye, was the *Almas*...a pure diamond whose colour was the flawless hue of a midnight desert sky shaped into a breathtaking heart. It radiated not just beauty, but magic, too.

It had been a long time since Zahir had even glanced at it, let alone studied it. But with its imagined connotations of visiting tragedy on his family he hardly needed to ask himself why. Hearing about the discovery of his great-great-grandmother's journal, and learning that the previous love-matches of his family had—as far as they were aware—been happy and successful, he now felt reassured to follow his heart.

Yet even if the history had not been good, Zahir knew it wouldn't have affected his decision... His arrogance had indeed diminished his wisdom when he'd sought to circumvent his destiny, but after his visit to Kajistan a few days ago, and hearing the wise thoughts of the Emir, he knew he would never be so foolish again as to think he even had a say in the matter.

'Oh, Zahir…' Turning towards him, Gina knew her lovely blue eyes glistened with tears. 'To be standing here, gazing at such an incredible sight… I feel utterly awed and privileged. Jake would have been beside himself to see the jewel as I am seeing it now.'

The sickening flash of jealousy that slashed through Zahir's insides was like having his legs kicked away from under him. 'Then how unfortunate that he so rashly decided to cut short his stay and go home,' he murmured, unable to keep the sarcasm from his voice.

'Yes…it was.' Her expression confused, Gina dipped her head.

'Are you sad that he left?'

Her head whipped up again. 'No! Why do you say that?'

'Because for you to mention that insignificant man at such an important time as this displeases me greatly, and it also has me thinking that perhaps you care for him more than you have admitted.'

'That's absolutely not true. He's a colleague—that's all. A colleague who worked as hard on researching the jewel as I did, and longed to view it for himself.'

'Then he should have stayed longer, instead of running away and insulting me by believing his very life was jeopardised by staying at the palace!'

His temper spilling over, Zahir stalked away from the cabinet to move across to the door. He could rationalise his emotionally charged response by telling himself he was still a little overwrought at all the events that had recently unfolded, but this was patently *not* the way he'd imagined the scene when he finally showed Gina the jewel and told her how he felt. A turbulent mix of anger as well as despair twisted his gut, and his mind took him down an even darker road.

'If it is not Jake you honour with your interest, what about the other men you must have met since we parted that night three years ago?'

'What other men?' The blue eyes widened indignantly, like dazzling twin lakes. 'I never had an intimate relationship with any other man except *you*, Zahir—not in three years. I already told you that.'

'Even so…my fear is that you are merely *saying* that so as not to disappoint me.'

'I wouldn't lie to you. I want you to know that after we were together that night even the mere thought of being with another man that way was repugnant to me.'

Zahir sucked in a steadying breath. To learn that Gina had been intimate with him and *only* him rocketed his previously sinking spirits to the moon and back. He ventured a smile. 'Can't you tell how jealous I have been at the idea you had slept with other men after surrendering your virginity to me? If I've handled it badly and offended you, I sincerely apologise.'

She crossed her arms in front of her chest and sighed. 'I accept your apology… But, like I said, after we were together I simply wasn't interested in any other man but you, Zahir. And while we're still on the subject of my colleague Jake,' she continued, 'he simply couldn't *help* being fearful. He's an urban man who lives alone, and he has had no experience of much other than his books and his work. There's an old church near where we work, and every time its clock chimes the hour he practically jumps out of his skin. It's just not in his nature to be brave, Zahir. He's not like you. Some people confront their fears head-on, and others find themselves retreating to protect themselves because they can't cope with anything shaking them up.

Are you going to condemn him for what is, after all, quite a common human weakness?'

Clenching his fists down by his sides, Zahir shook his head. '*You* didn't run away. You even bit the man who assaulted you to get away from him—yes, *bit* him—without knowing how he would react and possibly risking more harm to yourself!' Unable to contain the great tide of strongly felt emotion that washed over him, he moved swiftly back to Gina's side. 'I die a thousand deaths every time I relive that scene in my mind and imagine that you could have been killed or maimed for life.'

'But I *wasn't* killed or maimed.' Her plump lower lip trembled. Shakily she moved her hand to brush back her hair.

The tumult inside Zahir's chest slowly started to subside. But it was replaced by an even stronger emotion. He sighed. 'I am in awe of your incredible bravery…at what you did that day. Not one in a hundred women would have had the presence of mind to do what you did. Not to put too fine a point on it, the man who attacked you is a trained fighter…a mercenary. He lives high in the mountains, where he and his brother believe themselves to be outside the realms of any civilised law made to curtail their more base instincts and reckless activities. Yet, not knowing the danger, you fought back. You are quite a remarkable woman, Gina Collins.'

'Not really,' she murmured softly, gazing up at him. 'But sometimes…sometimes certain strong feelings can give you the courage to be stronger.'

'And what strong feelings would those be…hmm?'

'When you—when you care for someone deeply you don't want to leave them…you want to stay with them for the rest of your life, and you'll do anything you can to prevent being parted. I truly regret not coming back to you three years ago, but when my mother died I was over-whelmed with fear. I wasn't courageous enough to trust that it was right to return. When my father put doubts in my head about it, I listened to him rather than to my heart. It's true what they say, you know…about what happens when you're in serious danger. My life *did* flash before me when that man grabbed me at the marketplace, and I promised myself in that same moment that if I survived I would tell you exactly how I feel.'

Zahir stilled, yet his heart thudded hard. 'You said that gazing at the jewel made you feel awed and privileged. I could say the same thing about looking at you, *rohi*.' His voice was now helplessly infused with the warmth that was growing powerfully inside him. Tenderly, gently, he laid his palm against her cheek. 'I want to hear what you have to say, my angel. But first I have a question. There is an inscription on the back of the jewel's fastening…do you know what the translation of it is?'

Her smile was instantaneous, but shy. 'I could recite it in my sleep,' she confessed. 'It means *Transcend fear to find the courage to follow your heart and love without reservation.* I know I've had to do just that, Zahir.'

'And my heart echoes it.' Moving his hands to the small, feminine waist he could span with just his hands, Zahir drew Gina towards him, his blood pounding through his veins like a turbulent river as he examined her exquisite features and shining eyes. She was like rare perfume, or some intoxicat-ing elixir that he had inadvertently drunk—he would never get over the effects…*not as long as both of them lived and breathed.*

'Yes, my beloved… For a while I confess that I could not find the courage to love you unreservedly—not as long as I feared losing you. In my confused thinking I thought if I made you my mistress that would be a way of keeping you here, but at the same time I would not have to completely surrender my heart. It was the most colossal self-deception. Having found you again, I realised that to live without you would be the worst pain I could ever envisage. It is simply not an option. From the first moment I saw you, it never was. I love you, Gina. I want you not just because you are an incredibly beautiful and lovely woman and I desire you, I want you as my friend and companion as well as my lover...I want you to be my *wife*.'

Was she dreaming? Gina thought dazedly. Had her longing for this man at last turned her mind to madness? But, no, Zahir's love was blazing down at her like a fierce undaunted sun that would never set. She wanted to bask in that sun for the rest of her life.

'Are you sure, Zahir?' she asked quietly, afraid even at this incredible longed-for moment that she might somehow have misheard or misread him.

His glance was definitely perplexed. 'Am I *sure?*' he echoed in disbelief. 'I have just told the loveliest girl in the world that I want her to be my wife and she asks me that? Of *course* I am sure. Never again will I speak anything but the truth where my feelings for you are concerned.'

'It's just that right now I feel like I've somehow wandered into a dream. Nothing looks remotely the same any more. Everything has a celestial light shining on it. Seeing the jewel at last, and...' She lowered her lashes, overcome with shyness all of a sudden. 'I've dreamt of being with you, of becoming your wife for so long. Since that very first time we met, in fact. I knew then that you were the one I'd been waiting for all my life. But when I came back to Kabuyadir to find that you were ruler of the kingdom, no less... Well, I thought I had been dreaming a dream that was totally impossible. Forget it, I told myself. But I couldn't… I *couldn't*—because I love you so much. You mean the world to me, you know.'

He tipped up her chin so that she could not mistake the love that poured from his eyes…from his *heart* into hers.

'I told you when we first met that I had never felt as strongly about a woman before—as if she were a part of me that I never even knew I had lost until I met her… I still feel that way. In fact the feeling has deepened beyond measuring. But when you came back to Kabuyadir I was a different man from the one who spent that incredible night with you, Gina. After my father died, and then my sister's husband, I lost faith in love. All I seemed able to see was the pain it caused—because if you loved someone it was *beyond* agony when you lost them. I didn't want to suffer that pain again if I could help it. So I thought to bypass love completely. I fooled myself that I could marry purely to make an alliance that would benefit the kingdom. But I was wrong…*so* wrong. Just seeing you again taught me that. There are no words to describe how much your love for me thrills and fulfils me. Of all the things I have achieved it is your love, *rohi,* that will always be my greatest achievement.'

'You have called me that from the beginning…*rohi.* What does it mean, Zahir?'

He pressed a lingering warm kiss to her delectable lips, then gently drew away. 'It means "my soul" and that is what you have become.'

'I love that,' she breathed on a wistful sigh. 'I love the way that word sounds on your lips. I will *always* love it.'

'Well?' Reaching behind her head, Zahir opened the clasp that held her hair back, then threaded his fingers through the silken gold locks that tumbled unhindered onto her shoulders.

'Well, what?'

'I have just asked you to be my wife, have I not? I would very much like to hear your answer.'

'Yes!' Her arms went lovingly and firmly round his waist, and although her tight embrace made him wince because of the still tender wound at his side, Zahir had no intention of asking her to ease it. 'Yes, yes, *yes,*' she uttered passionately. 'A thousand times yes!'

She moved over him in the flickering shadows reflected by the burning candle in the lamp, and her skin was pale as new milk and softer than the finest silk. Zahir released a groan that scraped over gravel as he thrust up high inside her, his sex hardening like hot steel.

'I love you,' he murmured as he filled his hands with her velvet-tipped breasts. 'I love what you do to me... I love how you make me feel.'

Gina's bewitching blue eyes smiled provocatively down at him in the half-light of the Bedouin tent, her unbound hair gleaming gold fire across her pale slender shoulders. 'How *do* I make you feel? Tell me—and you can be as poetic and romantic as you like, my love.'

'Poetry right now is perhaps a tall order.' His aroused grin was rueful. 'But being inside you like this makes me feel like I'm going to die from the sheer pleasure of you, my Sheikha.'

'Sheikha...doesn't that mean the Sheikh's wife?'

'It does.'

'But I'm not your wife yet, Zahir.'

His hands fell to her softly rounded hips and cupped them possessively. 'But you soon will be,' he declared fiercely, emotion making him thrust harder.

'Oh, my...' She shut her eyes, as if to fully absorb the power of their incredibly passionate union, then opened them again to gently rock her hips forward and back. 'I soon will be.'

'And soon after that…' He held her still for several moments, so that he was acquainted with her body more intimately than he had ever believed possible, until he felt every pulse and contraction inside her as though they were his own. They had literally become one—together and indivisible—in a true connection that was not just of the body but of the heart and the spirit, too. The sensation was definitely transcendent.

'Didn't anyone ever tell you to finish your sentences? *Ohh!*' Gina's head fell back as her climax burst upon her, carrying her away to a state of bliss he was eager to join her in. She had never looked more radiant.

'Soon after we are married you will be carrying my child, *rohi*.' Zahir's fingers curled into the soft flesh of her hips as he deliberately kept her exactly where she was. Seconds later his seed spilled hot and unconstrained inside her.

CHAPTER TWELVE

GINA had hardly been able to stop shivering all day. But it was excitement not fear that had given her tremors. From the moment she had seen Zahir in his magnificent black and gold robes, looking like a powerful warrior from ancient times, from the moment she had uttered her vows in taking him as her husband, and from their entry into the palace's grand hall for the reception afterwards, where a huge gathering of friends and extended family waited to greet them, she had been beside herself with joy.

But there was one guest she was anticipating seeing more than anyone else. Her father Jeremy had flown in from London late the night before, and apart from greeting him enthusiastically and making sure he had everything he needed she hadn't really had a chance to talk to him yet.

He had not arrived unaccompanied. With him he had brought his new housekeeper Lizzie Eldridge, and now, when Gina saw him waiting patiently, away from the tight knot of well-wishers and friends who waited to greet the bride and groom, she noticed with a small leap inside her stomach that he was holding the attractive brunette's hand... holding it rather *possessively,* too.

Leaving Zahir's side, Gina rushed over to him. Opening his arms, her father tightly embraced her. *Was that a new aftershave he was wearing?* He looked very smart, dressed in a trim ecru-coloured suit, and his greying hair had had a decent cut, she noticed. Was this Lizzie's doing? Clearly the woman had wrought more changes in his life than simply easing the burden of housework for him. Gina was more than glad. She knew now that she loved her father dearly, and more than anything she wanted the second half of his life to be as fulfilling as the first had been with her mother.

'You look utterly radiant, my darling—like a princess from the court of one of the caliphs,' Jeremy enthused, still gripping her hand when their embrace was over. 'Does your young prince of the desert know how lucky he is?'

Gina gasped as Zahir came up behind her and drew her back against him. She adored it when he held her like that. Sensing his hard, indomitable male strength made her feel safe, loved and protected.

'He does indeed, Professor Collins. Believe me, I count my blessings every day that I have found the greatest love of my life, and I thank you from the bottom of my heart for giving her to me in marriage.'

Flushing a little, the older man smiled. 'Just take good care of her, will you? She means a lot to me...always has and always will. During her growing up I was sometimes remiss in telling her that I loved her, but now that I'm older and wiser, and have realised what a great gift she is, I hope I can make up for that.'

'You will always find a welcome here at the palace,' Zahir told him warmly.

Feeling her throat swell tightly, Gina leaned forward and kissed her father on his cheek. 'I love you, too, Dad... very much.'

When she stepped back, Zahir drew her possessively to his side again, as if staking his claim and saying, *I'm the one who will take care of her now.*

'Many congratulations to you both.'

The expression in Lizzie Elridge's clear grey eyes was a little nervous for a moment, and who could blame her? One minute she was in London, housekeeping for a professor still grieving for his wife, then the next she was in Kabuyadir, at the wedding reception of an imposing sheikh and the very ordinary British girl he incredibly wanted to marry! If Lizzie were in her shoes, she would wonder if she hadn't inadvertently rubbed Aladdin's lamp while she was doing her household chores and conjured up a scene from a fairytale.

'Thank you,' Gina and Zahir replied at the same time.

'And I'd just like to say thanks to you, Lizzie, for helping my dad,' added Gina. 'I feel so much happier being away from him knowing that he has someone like you in his life, helping take care of him.'

'You're more than welcome. Your dad's made such a difference to my life, and my son's, too, Gina. The truth is I never trusted men very much until I met Jeremy, so us getting along so well has been a lovely revelation to me. He's a real gentleman, your dad is.' Beneath the carefully applied blusher she'd applied to her softly plump cheeks Lizzie blushed even more. 'And if you're ever worried about him, please don't hesitate to call me and have a chat.'

'I will.'

'Did you have that sensational outfit specially made?' the older woman asked, politely changing the subject and gently touching her fingers to the red, bronze and burnt ochre-coloured silk skirt and matching jewel-encrusted fitted jacket that made up Gina's bridal dress.

'I did, yes.'

'Well, it's absolutely gorgeous. You look just like a goddess.'

'Thanks, Lizzie... I don't know about a goddess, but I

must admit I feel a little like royalty in this outrageously glamorous ensemble. I've promised my husband I won't let it go to my head!'

'You are allowed to behave like royalty on your wedding day, *rohi*. because that's what you are. And, knowing you, you will very quickly revert back to the shy, unassuming, but secretly *feisty* Gina I adore.'

'Would you call me feisty, Dad?'

'You're your mother's daughter, Gina. Charlotte was a dedicated academic, but that doesn't mean to say that she was boring, or didn't have a temper, or didn't like to have her own way from time to time.'

'Oh…'

'That took the wind out of your sails, my princess, didn't it?' Zahir grinned.

Gina made a face at him.

After that, the couple were drawn away by other patiently waiting well-wishers—first and foremost Farida. For their wedding, and at Zahir's carefully worded request, she had eschewed her familiar black dress for a set of midnight-blue regal robes, and with her elfin face and glossy dark hair caught up high behind her head she was the one, in Gina's eyes, who appeared every inch the royal princess.

'Gina—my dear, dear sister.'

The two women hugged affectionately, and when they broke apart, it was Zahir's turn to be embraced.

'I was wrong about the Heart of Courage, my sister.' He smiled fondly. 'And you were right about it being a blessing all along. I swear to you I will never again think of getting rid of it. In future I will listen to the wisdom of the women in my life where such important matters are concerned, rather than riding roughshod over their opinions.'

'If you do that, my brother, then you will indeed be a truly wise ruler!'

'Pardon me…' A slim, dark-haired man with the most intense ebony eyes presented himself.

'Masoud!' Zahir embraced his friend fondly.

When he was set free again, the man turned his gaze on Gina. 'Your love and beauty have transformed my friend His Highness into the happiest of men.' He smiled. 'I would like to thank you for that. There is no man who deserves the joy you bring more.'

'Thank you, Masoud. I know that your friendship means a lot to Zahir and always will.'

Late into the night, when the party was over and the guests had disbanded, Gina and Zahir drank aromatic coffee with Farida, Gina's father and Lizzie in one of the many beautiful salons that abounded in the palace. Together they reflected on the incredibly happy event that had taken place that day.

Snuggled up next to her new husband on a sumptuous couch, pleasantly tired and secretly longing for the moment when they could retire to bed together, Gina reflected on how happy it had made Zahir to be reacquainted in a much more joyful scenario with his friends Amir and Masoud. He was so loyal and devoted to those he cared about that she was certain they all felt blessed to count him not just as their ruler, but as a firm and constant friend, too.

Seated opposite them in the intimate arrangement of seats, her father leant forward from the gold-coloured embossed couch he shared with Lizzie to address Kabuyadir's handsome and impressive ruler. 'Sheikh Kazeem Khan—' he began politely.

Next to Gina, her husband held up his hand. 'Call me Zahir,' he said. 'You are my father-in-law now, and I do not want formality to be a barrier to our friendship.'

'Zahir,' Jeremy Collins said, an embarrassed little quirk

to his lips, 'I hope I am not being presumptuous by raising the topic right now, but I was wondering if you might
in the future consider bringing the Heart of Courage to
London. Perhaps to be exhibited in the British Museum?
I have no doubt it would excite much interest amongst not
only historians and those interested in ancient artefacts but
in the general public, too. Especially because of the way it
inadvertently brought you and my daughter together.'

'What do you think, Gina?'

She was a little taken aback when her handsome husband
asked her opinion. Clearly this was a new side to him that
she would have to get used to. He had barely let go of her
hand since the ceremony, and even now, as they sat informally with family, he still held it. Glancing into the gaze
that definitely reflected the tender feelings of his heart on
this most special of all the days since they had met, Gina
nodded lightly. 'I agree with my dad that it would definitely
excite interest. But the point is…would you be prepared
to bring it to London to be shown, Zahir? It is, after all, a
family heirloom first and foremost.'

'Why not?' He touched his palm gently to her cheek.
'It might be nice to go to London in a few weeks' time,
when it can be arranged. We still haven't reached a solution
about a honeymoon because you will not make a decision
on where to go.'

'I like it here,' Gina confessed, dimpling, 'I like it so
much that I don't want or need to go anywhere else for quite
a while.'

'Well, if we go to London you can show me the sights
and give me a personal guided tour. When I was at university in Oxford I was too fond of my studies to go there
very often. I confess I have a great desire to experience the
view from the top of the London Eye.' He turned back to

his father-in-law. 'So, my answer to your question is, yes, Jeremy. I *would* be prepared to take the jewel to London.'

Gina and Zahir—accompanied by a sturdily built palace bodyguard—swept by the eager queue that had formed outside the small private gallery where the Heart of Courage was making its much anticipated debut. With her handsome attentive husband holding her hand all the way, Gina felt as if she was on the set of a movie—her role that of the very fortunate heroine, and Zahir's the devastatingly gorgeous and strong hero. Every female in the audience would breathe a collective sigh of longing when they saw him.

The whole scene had a very dreamlike quality to it, but in truth all she had to do was glance up into Zahir's mesmerising dark gaze to learn that it was no dream or illusion. It was real, and it was true.

They had been married for three months now, and every day and night felt like a honeymoon. Every morning when she woke up in their bed, either in the palace or in the beloved Bedouin tent that they continued to visit often, Gina would find some exquisite gift left by her husband on her pillow—each one more beautiful and precious than the last.

Now, as she stood beside him to gaze again at the breathtaking jewel that had brought them together, arranged in pride of place at the centre of a collection of ancient Persian artefacts that included items from both temples and tombs as well as from royal houses, Gina found herself pulled gently against Zahir's side. Dressed in his now familiar robes, his luxuriant hair loose round his powerful shoulders, as he wore it in Kabuyadir, he might have been some dark exotic bird in the middle of an aviary of sparrows, she thought, smiling. Such was his imposing presence. The head curator of the gallery, a tall, slim redhead with glasses, looked as if she'd won the Lottery every time Zahir so much as glanced her way.

When they turned round, there was a bank of photographers, eager to take their pictures—Zahir, Gina and the famous jewel. With no time to prevaricate, Gina tugged her husband's hand to get his attention.

'What is it?' he whispered urgently, his intense dark gaze mirroring faint alarm.

'I'm pregnant.'

'What?'

'I was going to tell you tonight at dinner, but suddenly I…' She felt herself blush hotly. 'Suddenly I just couldn't wait.'

'Are you sure? How long have you known this?'

'I've been having symptoms for a while now, but I didn't want to say anything in case I was wrong. I'm about eleven weeks along…so Dr Saffar thinks.'

'My own physician knew about this before I did?'

'Don't look so put out,' Gina teased, brushing an imaginary speck from the front of his dark blue robes. 'Of course he knew before you. He's *my* doctor as well now—remember?'

Zahir shook his head. He was trying to pretend he was annoyed, but the edges of his well-cut lips kept tugging upwards and betrayed him. 'You are a little minx, giving me this news at such an awkward time.'

'Why is it awkward?'

'Well, if you don't mind me demonstrating my pleasure to you in front of an audience of interested strangers, then just say the word.' He purposefully lowered his head towards her, and there was a distinctly lascivious gleam in his eye.

Gina put her hand against his chest to stop him. 'Perhaps this isn't the best time,' she agreed, feeling suddenly hot.

Zahir's expression turned serious for a moment, prompting her to hurriedly enquire, 'You don't mind…about the baby, I mean?'

'Mind? You know it is the news I have dreamt about hearing ever since you agreed to be my wife—the news every man who loves the woman in his life beyond reason hopes to hear… But you certainly know how to choose your moments, my love!'

'Well…' She let him tug her closer into his side. 'You delight in surprising *me*…now it's my turn. So you're pleased, then?'

She almost held her breath as his glance became serious again. Yes, she knew how much it meant to him for them to have a child together, and wanted it as earnestly as Zahir, but sometimes the doubts of the past would occasionally surface and threaten to take away her happiness. Bit by bit she'd resolved to ignore those doubts and simply dwell on her good fortune instead and be glad.

Zahir was smiling warmly down at her again, and the depth of that incredible smile chased away all Gina's doubts. When her husband utilised that smile it was as though blazing sunshine appeared from behind a bank of stormy grey clouds and lit up the world.

'Pleased?' he answered. 'I am almost speechless with happiness. I just have to take it in for a moment. How you now expect me to give a talk about the Heart of Courage after hearing such news, I do not know.'

'You'll be fine.' Grinning mischievously, Gina stood on tiptoe to plant a tender kiss at the side of his mouth. 'You faced a horde of unruly rebels without a blink… If you can do that then you can easily talk about your family heirloom to a crowd of curious visitors. It'll be a piece of cake!'

'Sheikh Kazeem Khan!' someone called out from

behind them. 'Can we have a picture of you and your lovely sheikha now?'

They turned together to face the sea of flash-popping cameras. Zahir slipped his arm protectively round his wife's still slim waist. 'The sooner we return to Kabuyadir and relative anonymity, the better I will like it,' he whispered low in Gina's ear.

She glanced up at him and her blue eyes were infinitely tender, and somewhat teasing, too. 'Even if you weren't the Sheikh of the kingdom, you couldn't be anonymous if you tried, Zahir. You're far too imposing for that!'

'Imposing, but friendly,' he joked, and kissed her there and then on the lips, for everyone to see...

* * * * *

CLASSIC

Quintessential, modern love stories
that are romance at its finest.

COMING NEXT MONTH from Harlequin Presents®
AVAILABLE FEBRUARY 28, 2012

**#3047 A SHAMEFUL
CONSEQUENCE**
The Secrets of Xanos
Carol Marinelli

**#3048 AN OFFER SHE
CAN'T REFUSE**
Emma Darcy

**#3049 THE END OF
HER INNOCENCE**
Sara Craven

**#3050 THE THORN IN
HIS SIDE**
21st Century Bosses
Kim Lawrence

**#3051 STRANGERS IN
THE DESERT**
Lynn Raye Harris

**#3052 FORBIDDEN TO
HIS TOUCH**
Natasha Tate

COMING NEXT MONTH from Harlequin Presents® EXTRA
AVAILABLE MARCH 13, 2012

**#189 THE SULTAN'S
CHOICE**
Sinful Desert Nights
Abby Green

**#190 GIRL IN THE
BEDOUIN TENT**
Sinful Desert Nights
Annie West

**#191 TROUBLE IN A
PINSTRIPE SUIT**
Men Who Won't Be Tamed
Kelly Hunter

**#192 CUPCAKES AND
KILLER HEELS**
Men Who Won't Be Tamed
Heidi Rice

You can find more information on upcoming Harlequin® titles,
free excerpts and more at www.HarlequinInsideRomance.com.

HPECNM0212

REQUEST YOUR
FREE BOOKS!

2 FREE NOVELS PLUS
2 FREE GIFTS!

YES! Please send me 2 FREE Harlequin Presents® novels and my 2 FREE gifts (gifts are worth about $10). After receiving them, if I don't wish to receive any more books, I can return the shipping statement marked "cancel." If I don't cancel, I will receive 6 brand-new novels every month and be billed just $4.30 per book in the U.S. or $4.99 per book in Canada. That's a saving of at least 14% off the cover price! It's quite a bargain! Shipping and handling is just 50¢ per book in the U.S. and 75¢ per book in Canada.* I understand that accepting the 2 free books and gifts places me under no obligation to buy anything. I can always return a shipment and cancel at any time. Even if I never buy another book, the two free books and gifts are mine to keep forever.   106/306 HDN FERQ

Name	(PLEASE PRINT)

Address		Apt. #

City	State/Prov.	Zip/Postal Code

Signature (if under 18, a parent or guardian must sign)

Mail to the **Reader Service:**
IN U.S.A.: P.O. Box 1867, Buffalo, NY 14240-1867
IN CANADA: P.O. Box 609, Fort Erie, Ontario L2A 5X3

Not valid for current subscribers to Harlequin Presents books.

**Are you a current subscriber to Harlequin Presents books
and want to receive the larger-print edition?
Call 1-800-873-8635 or visit www.ReaderService.com.**

* Terms and prices subject to change without notice. Prices do not include applicable taxes. Sales tax applicable in N.Y. Canadian residents will be charged applicable taxes. Offer not valid in Quebec. This offer is limited to one order per household. All orders subject to credit approval. Credit or debit balances in a customer's account(s) may be offset by any other outstanding balance owed by or to the customer. Please allow 4 to 6 weeks for delivery. Offer available while quantities last.

Your Privacy—The Reader Service is committed to protecting your privacy. Our Privacy Policy is available online at www.ReaderService.com or upon request from the Reader Service.

We make a portion of our mailing list available to reputable third parties that offer products we believe may interest you. If you prefer that we not exchange your name with third parties, or if you wish to clarify or modify your communication preferences, please visit us at www.ReaderService.com/consumerschoice or write to us at Reader Service Preference Service, P.O. Box 9062, Buffalo, NY 14269. Include your complete name and address.

Harlequin *Presents*

USA TODAY bestselling author

Carol Marinelli

begins a daring duet.

THE SECRETS
of
XANOS

*Two brothers alike in charisma and power;
separated at birth and seeking revenge...*

Nico has always felt like an outsider. He's turned his back on his
parents' fortune to become one of Xanos's most powerful exports
and nothing will stand in his way—until he stumbles
upon a virgin bride....

Zander took his chances on the streets rather than spending another
moment under his cruel father's roof. Now he is unrivaled in
business—and the bedroom! He wants the best people around him,
and Charlotte is the best PA! Can he tempt her
over to the dark side...?

A SHAMEFUL CONSEQUENCE
Available in March

AN INDECENT PROPOSITION
Available in April

New York Times *and* USA TODAY *bestselling author*
Maya Banks presents book three in her miniseries
PREGNANCY & PASSION.

TEMPTED BY HER INNOCENT KISS

Available March 2012 from Harlequin Desire!

There came a time in a man's life when he knew he was well and truly caught. Devon Carter stared down at the diamond ring nestled in velvet and acknowledged that this was one such time. He snapped the lid closed and shoved the box into the breast pocket of his suit.

He had two choices. He could marry Ashley Copeland and fulfill his goal of merging his company with Copeland Hotels, thus creating the largest, most exclusive line of resorts in the world, or he could refuse and lose it all.

Put in that light, there wasn't much he could do except pop the question.

The doorman to his Manhattan high-rise apartment hurried to open the door as Devon strode toward the street. He took a deep breath before ducking into his car, and the driver pulled into traffic.

Tonight was the night. All of his careful wooing, the countless dinners, kisses that started brief and casual and became more breathless—all a lead-up to tonight. Tonight his seduction of Ashley Copeland would be complete, and then he'd ask her to marry him.

He shook his head as the absurdity of the situation hit him for the hundredth time. Personally, he thought William Copeland was crazy for forcing his daughter down Devon's throat.

Ashley was a sweet enough girl, but Devon had no desire

to marry anyone.

William had other plans. He'd told Devon that Ashley had no head for the family business. She was too softhearted, too naive. So he'd made Ashley part of the deal. The catch? Ashley wasn't to know of it. Which meant Devon was stuck playing stupid games.

Ashley was supposed to think this was a grand love match. She was a starry-eyed woman who preferred her animal-rescue foundation over board meetings, charts and financials for Copeland Hotels.

If she ever found out the truth, she wouldn't take it well.

And hell, he couldn't blame her.

But no matter the reason for his proposal, before the night was over, she'd have no doubts that she belonged to him.

What will happen when Devon marries Ashley?
Find out in Maya Banks's passionate new novel
TEMPTED BY HER INNOCENT KISS
Available March 2012 from Harlequin Desire!